IMPERIAL SECRETS

RECIPES WORTH DYING FOR

IMPERIAL SECRETS

RECIPES WORTH DYING FOR

PAUL BRENNAN

Troubador Publishing Ltd
Unit E2 Airfield Business Park,
Harrison Road, Market Harborough,
Leicestershire LE16 7UL
Tel: 0116 279 2299
Email: books@troubador.co.uk
Web: www.troubador.co.uk

ISBN 978 1 8051 4353 6

British Library Cataloguing in Publication Data.
A catalogue record for this book is available from the British Library.

Printed and bound in Great Britain by 4edge Limited
Typeset in 11pt Minion Pro by Troubador Publishing Ltd, Leicester, UK

For Mum, Tracey, Ellie and Florrie.

1

THE TEMPLE OF DAWN

Sometimes history should be left in the past, where it belongs. Had she listened to that advice, Naz might not be floating face down in the swollen river, tethered to the ferry pier by her jacket. Nor would she have to suffer the indignity of gawping morning commuters crowding at the water's edge, each trying to get a good photo of her dead body for their social media feeds. Their usual route to work has been blocked by a priest from the nearby temple. He's chanting in prayer, surrounded by sweet-smelling smoke from the incense sticks burning in his clenched hands. If he's trying to absolve her of sin, he's got a lot of work to do.

Kris Kongsin's car is crawling down Wang Doem alley towards the pier, parting the crowd with its siren. He's feeling sorry for himself. He'd only just sat down at his desk when the call came in from the ferry company. Just enough time to grab a coffee and head over to the temple. What a great start to the day. He walks over to the railing where the priest is standing and pulls out a cell phone.

"Kongsin here. I need a recovery team; there's a body in the river. Temple of Dawn ferry pier, west bank. Yeah, *of course* it's dead. You think I'm doing this for a laugh? Tell them to get a move on, will you? There's a circus forming over here. I need to get the body back to the mortuary before the press catches wind. It'll be all over the web by now. Thanks, mate."

Two police officers run plastic incident tape across the entrance to the pier. Kongsin shouts at the crowd. "Come on, people, there's nothing for you to see or do here. Give us some room, will you? You can see what's happened. Let us do our job."

He talks to the priest. "You can stay if you wish until we've recovered the body," he says. The priest, still moving his mouth in prayer, turns his head and nods. By the time the police launch arrives, the sun is already burning through the morning mist and the din of morning river traffic is growing louder. One officer photographs the body in place before helping to haul her out.

Kongsin's cell phone rings.

"Chirapat Amudee here, sir. I'm down here with the body."

Kongsin looks over the edge of the pier and waves. "What have you got then?"

"Middle-aged woman, sir. Black hair. Blue jeans, black T-shirt. Rose gold Rolex on her right wrist. No rings. She's been shot in the head. Entrance wound in her left cheek, by the looks of it. Back of her head's missing. Looks nasty, sir. We'll take her over to the mortuary at Pathum Wan. See you there?"

When did a head shot ever look *nice*?

"Thanks, Amudee." Kongsin ends the call and lights an L&M with his father's old Zippo. He rests his forearms on the railing, blowing out smoke, scanning his eyes up the western bank of the river. The body must have been dumped up there somewhere. The killer would have assumed it would simply float out to sea. Idiot. Anyone local would know the currents here. Or maybe she shot her own head off. He takes a lung full, flicks the remains of his cigarette into the river, turns and walks back to the squad car.

He grunts at his driver. "Pathum Wan Station. Fast."

2

A MANUSCRIPT

The files have been sent up to the Asian and African reading room by one of the information specialists working in the British Library's subterranean archive. Sara has been unusually specific about this collection of papers from the Malacca archive, asking if they could be made available for five consecutive days. This isn't especially unusual for a PhD student; Sara has often spent many days examining single documents since starting her research. In a trance-like state of academic absorption she often completely overlooks the need to eat and drink and emerges famished and dry-mouthed into the evening traffic chaos of Euston Road, urgently seeking food and water. She enjoys the cavernous silence of the library, the hushed devotion to ancient texts, the joy of reading words written by another hand in another time that have lain quietly undisturbed for centuries. She loves the fact that history has a smell. Earthy, sour, exotic.

The Malacca archive had been shipped to London by the Government of the Straits Settlements following its discovery in the basement of the old court house in the Malaysian port town of Malacca by workmen in 1927. This minor archive hadn't been fully catalogued until the 1980s, and even now, the contents of almost one hundred stout boxes of assorted documents were largely unexplored: secrets perhaps, lost stories waiting to be revealed. Most of the records appeared to relate to either the Dutch or British East India Companies' activities in Malacca from the middle of the eighteenth century.

Today, London is awash with umbrellas, taxis and raised voices in the damp, grey gloom of a weekday morning. Inside the reading room, deep within the library's red-brick fortress walls, the atmosphere is warm and hushed. Sara sits at a large desk, onto which a shallow plastic tray has been placed. Inside, a reinforced cardboard archive box. On one end, a label typed in English on an old-fashioned typewriter reads: *R/9. Malacca Old Court House 1927 archive. Contents of Miscellaneous box 5. Status: catalogued.*

Four separate files have been placed inside the archive box. At the bottom, Sara finds the file she wants to inspect and lifts it carefully onto the tabletop. Two thick boards, marbled in blue and brown, once joined along one edge with a broad fabric tape that has long since disintegrated, feel cool and smooth. A small paper label, glued to the front cover with a handwritten note in faded copperplate ink under a printed crest, identifies the contents: *Zaak 1768/25. Onbekend Chinees Manuscript.* Dutch. A legal case, perhaps, from the old Court House in Malacca from the time of the Dutch East India Company occupation. The boards are held together with new linen ribbon, which Sara unties again with care. She slides a sheaf of parchment sheets from between the boards and slowly runs her fingers over the hand-stitched binding and thick, rippled pages.

The text had caught Sara's eye the previous afternoon, but it was late in the day and she wasn't able to study it in detail. This isn't European writing, nor Chinese, nor Malay for that matter, she decides. On the front page is some sort of map, under which, clearly written in an Arabic script, is a single phrase:

میر کاظمی

A title. A name, perhaps? She can't decipher it. Case number 25, archived in the year 1768, is clearly no ordinary manuscript from the colonies. She sits in silence in the empty reading room, hands clasped as if in prayer, staring down at her discovery, inhaling its history. Usually calm, focused and closed, Sara now feels her pulse race.

Tell me your story.

The wavy parchment pages crackle as Sara turns them with great care. On the front page, a map has been sketched in brown ink. It seems to show an island, surrounded by water channels. Rivers maybe, or a moat? On the island are depictions of buildings, oriental in style. Pagodas. Temples perhaps. A curious eight-sided building stands on one edge of the island, and boats – ships? – on the opposite side. There follow two pages of almost-unbroken text, then several more, each with the same format: a list, followed by paragraphs, often with ornate Arabic symbols and adjustments, corrections or notes, written in another hand in a red-brown ink. Sara photographs the island sketch and several sheets of text before carefully returning the documents to their archive box and returning them to the librarian for safekeeping.

A chill wind catches Sara by surprise as she leaves the Tube at Elephant and Castle just after 10pm. She turns and walks her usual route home along Borough High Street. She lives a quiet, intelligent life in a small, rented flat above an Asian supermarket, twenty minutes' walk from the station. In her life, there is little space for other humans. They're too distracting. Aside from her doting parents, she only really enjoys the company of two other people: Ting, the owner of the Win Hip Supermarket downstairs; and David Ingleby, her old undergraduate tutor in Political Science at the University of London, an intense, dishevelled character with a love of good wine and choral music.

This evening is different to most. She is desperate to share her news with Ting. Inside Win Hip, she walks past shelves of exotic Asian goods to a space at the back of the shop where Ting is sitting, idly eating a tangerine. She peels the scarf from her face.

"Ting! You'll never guess what."

"If I'll never guess what, why don't you just tell me!" laughs the wiry Cantonese woman, almost three times Sara's age. "Tea for Sara!" she barks over her shoulder through an open kitchen door.

"I've found something *very* interesting in the British

Library, Ting. I'm really excited about this – I think it's going to turn out to be a major discovery."

Ting's mother – time-worn, shrunken and slow – brings hot jasmine tea to a small plastic table. Sara talks excitedly as the tea is poured into small cups.

"I've been looking at some old documents that were found in the basement of the old law court in Malacca."

Ting raises an eyebrow in half-interest. She is used to Sara being excited about small academic discoveries, most of which are too esoteric to demand much attention. But she loves Sara's youthful enthusiasm and often feigns interest while she thinks of more practical matters like stock control or what to cook for supper.

"The fascinating thing is, Ting, there were hundreds of documents in that cellar, some dating back to the 1600s, all of them left by either the Dutch or British during their occupations."

"Ah, that colonial business. It all ends in tears, you know."

"Yes, but Ting – most of the documents were about commercial activity in Malacca in the times of the East India Companies. That's what I have been researching for my PhD."

Ting frowns a theatrical frown. "Sara, you are one crazy young woman if you find that interesting. Why don't you find a nice man and settle down with him instead?"

"Ting. *Really.*" Sara sips at her tea and continues urgently. "In amongst all this stuff were some boxes of random documents. Many of them aren't written in Dutch or English. Some of them look Malay, some of the oldest papers are in Portuguese, but there's this one archive folder…"

"Don't tell me – you found the lottery numbers?"

"No! God, this is hard work. But I think what I have found is just as exciting. I think it's really old and really important."

David Ingleby had realised Sara's potential shortly after she had started her undergraduate studies. A self-designed eccentric, he is Sara's complete opposite: he – the grandly titled Churchill Professor of Political Policy at the University of London – overweight, middle-aged, loud, yellow-toothed from coffee and merlot; she, slender, young, discrete, a big fan of mineral water. Both are fiercely intelligent.

One evening, after a guest lecture, Ingleby had asked Sara, "What are you going to do with that enormous brain of yours?"

"I'm thinking about a career in research, Professor," she had replied. "I think I'd like to find out more about the British Empire. I'd like to understand the impact of our business activities on the colonies."

Ingleby, startled, had spluttered into his Nescafé. "Wow, you've really thought about this, haven't you? I can safely say that no undergraduate has ever given such a precise answer to that question."

"Just watch me, Professor," Sara had said, picking up her rucksack and preparing to leave. "I'll find a way."

That evening – one he would come to remember for a long time – Ingleby had decided that he quite liked this shy young student. Few had ever made such an impression on him. He had watched Sara through the rain-streaked window of his office as she hurriedly crossed the courtyard to the university library two levels below, then picked up the phone and dialled an old friend.

"Bob. Dave Ingleby. How are you keeping?"

A cough on the end of the line. "Not so bad thanks, old lad. Still here, at least. To what do I owe the pleasure?"

"Bob, do you still curate the British Library?" Ingleby asked.

"Good God, no, David, that would be a truly mammoth task. There's a big team of us these days. I do Asian and African. Hilary does Humanities, there's someone for maps, science, rare books; it's all getting very specialised now. Why, may I ask?"

"I've found a diamond, Bob. A real uncut one, ready for polishing."

"Historian?"

"Well, she's no politician, Bob, but she understands political theory. She'll get a first-class honours with me without any great effort on my part. We were just chatting this evening and it's clear she already has a Great Plan. She wants to study the East India Company archives to understand the financial impact of the Empire in Malaysia. She's half Malaysian herself, apparently."

Ingleby had heard the familiar clink of ice down the phone as Bob Oakhurst took a swig of his London gin and slimline. "In that case, my dear boy, send her over. It sounds like she may be exactly the sort of person I've been hoping to meet since 1985."

A few days later, Sara had half-skipped across the British Library's cavernous, hushed foyer and taken the elevator to Bob Oakhurst's office on the second level. In later years she would always remember his arrival in a glide of old-fashioned British suave.

"Bob Oakhurst," he announced in his soft Oxfordshire accent. "And you must be Sara – how lovely to meet you. My old friend David Ingleby speaks very highly of you."

Sara jumped to her feet. "Dr Oakhurst, I'm so excited to meet you," she blurted.

"*Bob*, my dear. Everyone calls me Bob. It's too late in life to insist on anything else." Sara's outstretched hand disappeared into his large, warm, soft palm and he shook vigorously for slightly too long, Sara thought. His office was scented with tobacco and the familiar, musty taint of old manuscript. From his tweed-polished leather chair, Bob watched Sara scanning the room, wide-eyed. A large modern desk, bowed with files and papers, sat under a window through which Sara could make out the red-brick gothic of the St Pancras Hotel. Two walls were lined with shelves crammed with books, journals and files.

"I have become entombed, Sara. The past will envelope my tired body one day. There is no escape for me. I will have to be cremated *in situ*!" He laughed. "Do make yourself at home, although I suspect home isn't quite like this place. Tea?"

Sara politely declined and instead sipped from her water bottle. Oakhurst hung out of the office door and placed an order with his secretary before turning back to

Sara. "Assam in the afternoon, as a general rule. So, Sara, David tells me you have an idea about investigating the British Empire's financial abuse of its colonies."

"Well, I wouldn't necessarily put it like that," Sara replied, a little surprised.

"It's an interesting idea. Not unique, of course; the archives here contain a wealth of evidence – hidden between the lines, so to speak – that suggests we Brits took a few liberties in our overseas territories. As you know, most of that research concerns India, but we do have some excellent archives from other countries. You're Malaysian, David tells me?"

"Half. My mother is Straits Chinese, born in Penang, and my father is from Alnwick in Northumberland."

"How wonderful. Listen, I have an idea. In fact, I've had this idea for so long, I thought it would die with me. The Straits Settlements. In the early 1980s we got a whole new archive from the India Office Library over on Blackfriars Road, originally sent across to what we now call the Foreign Office many years ago. The records were retrieved from a city called Malacca in what became known as Malaysia."

"I know it well. When I was a young child, we went every year during the mid-autumn festival."

"*Really?* Now there's a thing. Well, no one has ever had the opportunity to have a good rummage through this archive. An old colleague – dead now, bless him – did a great cataloguing job back in the day but the fine detail is a complete mystery. It's been on my to-do list for over a decade. Of course, you'll know that Malacca was originally colonised by the Portuguese, then the Dutch, then the

British – so, if my hunch is correct, that archive should have all sorts of interesting information about commercial activity across at least two hundred years."

Sara realised what had just been laid at her feet and flushed. "That is exactly the sort of thing I would love to get stuck into, Bob."

"Then, Miss Richardson, I have a vacant, funded PhD post with your name on it. Just get your BA over with and give me a tinkle when you're ready."

Which is how the universe decided that Sara would discover Zaak 1768/25.

3

MORTUARY

9am. Kongsin arrives at the mortuary. A small crowd of journalists has already started to gather in front of the police station steps. "Great," Kongsin says to himself as he walks over to the mortuary entrance at the rear of the building. "Just what we need." He swipes his ID card and the door clicks open.

A broad man in pristine uniform greets him at the mortuary reception. Captain Nakul Chainarong. Shit. This is going to be a long day.

"DI Kongsin. Chainarong. Good to meet you."

"Of course, sir. Good to see you too. Is there a problem?"

"Well, you could say that, yes, Kongsin." He lowers his voice. "It's a very serious issue, in fact." He hands Kongsin a photo of the inscription on the back of the Rolex. The body is Nazia Khan.

Kongsin runs a hand through his hair and sighs heavily. "Ah, you're kidding, aren't you, sir? You're sure?"

Chainarong holds out a photograph of the body's face. "I'm perfectly sure, Detective Inspector."

"She's made so many enemies in this city, we'll never find out who did this." Kongsin reaches into his pocket for another L&M.

"I expect you to find the killer quickly, of course," Chainarong says. "You can imagine the media shitstorm this is going to create. I want you to keep me briefed day and night."

Kongsin enters the mortuary room where Nazia Khan's body is wide open on the dissection bench, her head propped on a wooden block. The pathology technician has just finished peeling her scalp forward to reveal the extent of the wound to her head. Kongsin winces and looks away. Who the hell would choose a job like that? He smears Tiger Balm under his nose and fits a face mask.

Joe Yunram notices his guest and strides across the mortuary floor, grinning. "Morning, Kris. This is pretty straightforward from my point of view," he says cheerfully, tapping a computer screen showing a set of X-ray images.

The Royal Thai Police's most annoying forensic pathologist, in Kongsin's opinion. Shame he happens to be on duty today; Kris can't stand the man.

"Looks like a close shot, Kris, but not point blank – there's not enough residue on the facial skin for that. Certainly close enough to blow the back of her brain out, though. Single shot from below, probably about minus thirty degrees. Some fresh bruising to her upper chest consistent with a blow, perhaps a shove or a forward fall onto something hard around the time she was shot. She will have been thrown backwards by this one, though.

There'll be a lot of splatter when you find the crime scene. Shoe tips scuffed, consistent with being dragged face-down when dead."

"Time of death?"

"Recent. Overnight. Probably about 2am, I'd guess."

"Weapon?"

"Not sure. Judging from the damage, it's a powerful weapon. Definitely a single bullet, fired from a pistol I expect. You find me the place of death and a bullet; I'll tell you what did this."

Kongsin smiles thinly under his mask. "Of course, Joe, that shouldn't take too long in this town…" he says. "I'll let you know what we turn up." He turns and leaves the mortuary, flicking his face mask into a bin by the door. A crowd of bored media people watch him walk from the building. They wake from their slumber and snap into action.

"Who is she?"

"Do you know who killed her?"

Kongsin stops, turns to the forest of cameras and notebooks and recites flatly, as he has on many previous occasions. "Ladies and gents, thank you for your interest. I can confirm that a body has been recovered from the Chao Phraya River this morning. We are currently identifying the body and beginning our investigations. As soon as we have some public interest news, we'll hold a formal press conference. Until that time, please allow us to proceed with our investigations uninterrupted. Thank you so much for your assistance."

Parasites.

4

BOB

Later that evening, Sara emails Bob Oakhurst.

From: *Sara Richardson >s.y.richardson@london.ac.uk*
To: *Bob Oakhurst >r.t.oakhurst@london.ac.uk*
Cc:
Date: *20.03.2020 22:23*
Att: *Archived_document_1.jpeg*
Subject: Unexpected document in Malacca archive

Bob, can I ask for your help? I found a document in the Malacca archive yesterday, filed by the Dutch as part of some sort of legal case (I'm presuming – it has a case number from 1768 and was found in a law court, so I think I am right on that).

I have attached an image of two pages. It looks as if it is written in some sort of Arabic script and there is a sketch, which could be a map or something. I could do with finding an expert in Arabic writing – do you know anyone?

I have no idea what this is doing in the East India Archives. Wouldn't it be good to know?

Thanks for your help, perhaps we can speak tomorrow?

SR

Bob, as usual, is working late in his office and hears Sara's email arrive. He opens the picture files and sits back in his chair, smiling to himself. *Here we go.*

From: Bob Oakhurst >r.t.oakhurst@london.ac.uk
To: Sara Richardson >s.y.richardson@london.ac.uk
Cc:
Date: 20.03.2020 22:35
Att:
Subject: Re: Unexpected document in Malacca archive

Sara

Now this is exciting! I don't know what it is but I have a good friend in Languages and Cultures of the Near and Middle East at SOAS. He's very discreet and we could ask him to offer an initial opinion.

I have been hoping that this archive would yield some interesting stuff. Let's see what Nasser says. I'll get back to you ASAP.

RTO

R T Oakhurst MA(Oxon) DPhil FRS
Chief Curator, African and Asian Archives
British Library

An hour has passed since Bob Oakhurst's speedy reply. Sara has tried to occupy her mind by emailing her parents to reassure them, as she does most days, that she is remembering to feed herself, drink occasionally and take exercise. She eats a meagre dish of instant noodles, tidies (there is nothing to tidy), writes a list of jobs (she has none) and paces the length of her flat.

The door buzzer buzzes. A hushed voice speaks on the intercom.

"Sara. It's Bob. Don't be alarmed. I need to speak to you. It's important."

Bob sits in Sara's small, sparsely furnished lounge and accepts the offer of tea. He seems excited, agitated almost. Sara places a mug on the side table next to him.

"Bob, I'm sorry, this is just standard teabag vintage. It's all I have. I'm not into that single estate stuff you like."

Bob smiles. "Thanks, Sara. I'm sure it'll be absolutely fine. Listen, let me get to the point. You must be wondering why I have come across to see you in person."

Yes, Sara thinks to herself, *this does feel a bit weird.*

"That manuscript. It's not really Arabic, Sara. It's *Persian*. Nasser Awad is sure of it. He's going to show one of his colleagues tomorrow morning. Someone called Morad."

"Persian? In Malacca?"

Oakhurst raises his eyebrows and grins. "Quite. Interesting, eh? Of course, the Persians had established trade links with Asia way before any Europeans did. Nasser has no idea what the map is but to me it looks like it must be somewhere in the Far East, not Iran. The buildings are pagodas, aren't they? Maybe temples. I think your document is much older than the rest of the archive, Sara. I think it's going to turn out to be very important. Don't suppose you have any wine?"

Sara laughs. "Wine? No, I've never tried it, Bob. I don't keep any drink in the house. I don't normally have anyone to share it with." Then, hardly changing pace, "I have always dreamed of a moment like this. A real discovery. Don't get me wrong, Bob, I'm enjoying my PhD and I really think I'm making a contribution to colonial studies – but it can be a bit dry. Not everyone's cup of tea." She blushes at her clumsy pun.

"Shame about the wine, Sara, I'm going to have to get you started. Some entry-level stuff perhaps. None of that posh stuff Ingleby likes. You'll enjoy it. Now listen, Sara, I need to say something to you. It might sound bonkers but I need you to agree to something for me." Oakhurst pauses, takes too much hot tea and winces before he continues. "On rare occasions we do make startling discoveries in our archives. We always will, I suppose, until we've read every document in there. Until we know exactly what this is, we need to remain absolutely shtum."

Sara nods.

"Nasser's a good lad," Oakhurst continues. "He's well aware of the potential implication of this discovery. He's not saying a thing. You and I need to publish this discovery as soon as we can. Until then I want to keep this under wraps. People spend their whole miserable academic careers hoping to find something like this. This is your baby, Sara; this could make your career."

Bob doesn't stay for much longer before he gives Sara an oversized corduroy hug and walks into the small hours of the morning to hail a passing taxi. Sara throws herself into her sofa and, for the first time in her adult life, screams. A high, free, happy scream. And then she stops, embarrassed at her loss of control.

5

7TH APRIL 1767

Mohamad was already awake when the sound of temple bells started to echo across the misted city walls and down its quiet streets. Most mornings, he would leave his wife and sons before sunrise and walk through streets filled with happy, familiar faces before presenting himself at the Imperial Court kitchens for work. This morning felt very different. He dressed quickly and went to stand outside. All around him, the narrow alleyways of the Muslim quarter appeared calm, save for the low chorus of bells.

Across the ancient Monkey Bridge, the Chinese market lay perfectly still. The surrounding canal waters sat undisturbed, green and mirror-like in the thin dawn light. Neighbours, also woken early, emerged from their shop-houses and gathered quietly near the bridge. It had started, finally.

Huge armies had assembled in the fields surrounding the city, building camps in drenching monsoon rains. For two years they had ruined lands to the north and south. Thousands of men, horses and elephant had crossed high mountain passes, spreading out across the plains of Siam, turning proud cities to ash and butchering their inhabitants. Terrible stories ran before them of families murdered in their homes, their children slaughtered as they played in the streets.

Here, the armies had met an ancient, moated city encircled by rivers in full flood. As the rains eased, the land had drained and hardened, allowing them to haul their cannon closer to the city's thick defensive walls. The siege had now lasted for over a year. Food supplies had dwindled to dust. Citizens fought over stale rice grains and rotten onions. Parts of the city had already been incinerated by incoming cannon fire, forcing whole families to live outside in open spaces. Women, sensing their fate, had cropped their hair and joined their husbands on the city walls, from where their own cannon echoed back across the plain. The Emperor, guided by his military advisors, had issued instructions for his war elephants to be taken from the city to safety, but had insisted that he and his family remained to face their enemy.

Overnight, with no moon to light them, the Burmese had built a causeway across the river to the foot of the Maha Chai fortress. Sappers armed with picks, shovels and wooden props had worked with ruthless speed over the previous week, digging deeply into the thick base of the fortress, packing their tunnel with pitch-soaked branches. In the thin morning light of 7th April, a single soldier marched across the causeway. His lighted torch etched an arc of flame across the darkness and into the tunnel entrance. A small group of holy men clad in golden robes gathered on the ramparts above to watch, their rhythmic chanting mixing with stinging smoke, now seeping upwards from the tunnel below them. In their midst, enrobed in fine silks and gilded armour plate, was their Emperor.

"Our holy city has seen these dogs before," he said to his advisors. "Today, we will defend our people. Much blood will be spilt upon our soil."

By mid-morning, the Maha Chai fortress walls had collapsed, cracking the city wide open. Squads of Burmese soldiers now poured across the causeway to murder a city already in panic.

Mohamad had rehearsed this moment in his mind for many months and knew instinctively what to do. He rushed to his family, shook them gently awake, wrapped his arms around them and kissed their heads.

"Azra, you must leave now," he whispered urgently to his wife. "Run quickly to the quayside by the Diamond Fort and jump onto any boat able to take you. Take the boys with you and leave. I must go to the monastery first but I will follow soon. It is my last duty here. I will come and find you."

He pushed a small leather purse of coins into Azra's

trembling hands. Her eyes met his and both filled with tears. She nodded, terrified. From the kitchen she took fruit and cooked rice before gathering her two young sons in her arms and leaving the house.

"I will find you!" Mohamad shouted after her, but she didn't reply. She knew he wouldn't. By the side of the canal, she joined terrified mothers and children running eastwards in the growing din. Brave husbands gathered weapons from their houses and ran together towards the city walls and certain death. Once-peaceful streets were now filled with the sound of fear.

Mohamad watched his family disappear from view, then turned and ran north past the merchant houses and shops lining the banks of the main canal. Families spilled out into open spaces, carrying whatever possessions they could gather in their arms, some pushing hand carts piled hopefully high with furniture. From the north, where smoke and flame danced behind the city's golden temple stupas, the crowd ran against Mohamad, crossing the city to reach the quays to the southeast.

As he turned towards the Royal Palace, Mohamad's heart heaved. Ahead, the Si Sanphet temple – the city's sacred Imperial burial place – was already alight. Huge orange flames danced mockingly through the tiled roof, licking its carved decorations, splitting its great teak beams and melting metal. The Royal Chapel's roof had already collapsed inwards. Across the blazing pillared hall and fallen roof timbers, the great golden Buddha's face glowed, seemingly unaware of his fate.

A group of monks had assembled in the inferno to kneel in front of their Buddha in frantic prayer, hands raised to the heavens. As they chanted, a squad of Burmese soldiers struck them from behind, bringing down their war scythes upon the monks' heads with such force that each was beheaded in an instant. Mohamad stopped and watched in disbelief, fell to the ground and prayed for salvation. As the soldiers ran laughing on towards the Royal Palace, he sprang to his feet and pushed on. Fear fuelled his body as he ran, crouched, along the Granary canal. On this spot, seven years before, another Burmese siege had been brought to a bloody end by the might of Siamese cannon and the charge of fearless war elephants – but there were none here today as Mohamad finally reached the Royal Garden monastery.

All was quiet among the funerary relics of past queens. A lone, elderly monk stood calmly at the monastery gate, leaning on a long bamboo pole.

"Ah, Mohamad, my dear friend," he said. "Do you not see the danger you have placed yourself in?"

"Holy father, I have come to collect my family's treasures. Only then can I leave."

"I understand," the monk replied. "Do what you must do. But be fast, my friend. The demon approaches."

The monk stood aside, allowing Mohamad into the monastery compound. Arranged around a central golden stupa stood four small halls built with red lacquered timber pillars, each crowned with a curved roof of ochre-glazed tiles. On the western side was the monastic reading room: here, precious, handwritten texts were stored in ornately decorated wooden chests arranged around a low, central platform where monks could sit and read. Inside the hall, the noise of cannon fire was muffled to almost perfect silence. Mohamad rested briefly. At the far end of the hall, thick with dust, was a black cabinet, richly painted with gilded images of the Buddha, its doors turned to the west.

Over a century before, Mohamad's ancestors had arrived from Persia after a long and arduous journey across the Bay of Bengal and through the mountainous lands of western Siam. Here they had sought a safe location, as close to their Holy City of Mecca as possible, to keep two ancient manuscripts, the Mirkazemi family's ancestral treasures. One was a fragment of the Qur'an, written in ornate Persian script on fine parchment. The abbot had agreed that it could be stored in the reading room at his monastery to honour its great age and holiness and provide a place where it could never be disturbed.

Mohamad pulled the cabinet from the wall. Inside, wrapped in a fragile gold-embroidered cloth, the two manuscripts were all that connected Mohamad to his ancestors. He lifted them with great care, whispering in prayer while he wrapped them in rush matting and placed them into a goatskin bag.

"Venerable sir," he said to the monk as he reached the gate again. "Our city is in flames. You can't stay here. Please, come with me. I will take you to safety."

The monk smiled. "My dear friend," he said, "I am old and frail, but my spirit is still strong. Whatever happens to this place, I must remain. The Imperial Household would expect it of me and it is my final purpose in this life. I will protect the spirits of the queens buried in this holy soil.

You are young, with much to live for. Go. Find your family and find peace." He held out his hands, which Mohamad gripped, and they both cried briefly, the monk with joy and Mohamad with terrible fear.

Mohamad turned to leave, his face bronzed by the burning palace to his left. Ash fell around them like large snowflakes. "Goodbye, dear friend," he said. "May your Lord protect you." He retraced his steps and stopped after a while to glance over his shoulder. The old monk still stood at the monastery gates, leaning on his pole, the golden stupa gleaming behind him. Within an hour he would be slain where he stood and the monastery set ablaze, its holy relics and royal graves plundered for their gold.

6

PERSIA

From: Bob Oakhurst >r.t.oakhurst@london.ac.uk
To: Sara Richardson >s.y.richardson@london.ac.uk
Cc:
Date: 22.03.2020 12:10
Att:
Subject: Unexpected document in Malacca archive

Sara. Great news. Morad's had a look and says it's definitely Persian. God knows what it's doing in the Malacca archive! We'll need a copy of the whole document so Morad can give us a translation. I have asked one of the archive assistants to help. Can you get it across to the photo lab urgently so I can have digital images by noon tomorrow? Please ask Mary to get a slot in my diary for later.

*   Best*
*   RTO*
R T Oakhurst MA(Oxon) DPhil FRS
Chief Curator, African and Asian Archives
British Library

P.S. I've also asked Mary to give you a bottle of cheap plonk from my secret stash. Remember to ask her.

7

COFFEE

11am. Kongsin drains a paper cup of strong black coffee, pauses to allow it to take effect, then turns to the assembled team.

"Right," he says, "this is *not* the sort of day you dream of. One of the most famous women in Bangkok has been shot in the head, then dumped in the river. The motive? Well, just about everyone hated her, so that narrows it down to a couple of million suspects."

Laughter.

"Weapon? A pistol of some sort. We don't know what yet. Place of death? We don't know that either yet. So, my friends, we have a lot of work to do. I need you to get serious. Every eye in the country is watching us. We have to find out who did this and we have to find out fast. I want to know if *anyone* within a mile of Wat Arun heard anything or saw anything between about two and six this morning. Get out there. Talk to people. We need a lead. We'll meet again at 5pm."

8

ESCAPE

He was surrounded by the heat and roar of destruction. A thick, slate smoke now shrouded the city from the sun. Ash cloaked its streets in grey drifts, stifling sound. Mohamad turned south, past the Monastery of the Moon, its intricately carved roof now burning. Enemy soldiers – children, mostly – rested briefly, laughing and sharing stories before they continued their murderous rampage. As Mohamad slipped unseen over the boundary wall, the temple's glorious, tiled roof collapsed inward in a huge, deafening cloud of black smoke and bright cinders. Ancient Chan trees lit like funeral torches, hot wind carrying their crimson flames into the next monastery compound to begin a new cremation.

Mohamad vaulted back into Moor Street and pushed on, his breath now scorched, wood smoke stinging his eyes. The air here reeked of burnt flesh and fear. Ahead of him, the path lay abandoned. Its once splendid temples lay ruined, prayer halls shattered, precious statues beheaded and toppled. As he reached the Muslim quarter again, all was silent; the merchants were gone, their proud homes ransacked, looted, their women taken. Mohamad's thoughts turned again to Azra and their precious sons. Tears streaked his ash-crusted face as he imagined their fate. His mind replayed Azra's wide brown eyes betraying her terror as she gathered the children in her arms.

"Azra!" he shouted soundlessly into the din around him, "I am coming for you!" But Azra did not hear.

Passing half-familiar streets and houses, he finally reached the Chinese quarter. Here, sugar, rice, sago, sandalwood and rattan once passed through the merchant warehouses lining the quays to the south and east. Here, too, generations of artisans had crafted fine furniture from precious hardwoods, lacquer work for the rich, temple goods cast in tin, bronze and gold. Fire had not yet reached there. The sounds of life had now been forced from its narrow alleyways, replaced by the rhythmic, dull pounding of Siamese cannon fire.

At the end of China Street, the Diamond Fortress had held circling Burmese troops at bay all morning. There, a frail old woman stood in the doorway of what was once her family's general store. She inspected Mohamad calmly as he walked up to her, holding his hands in front of his chest in prayer, his head bowed.

"It is all finished," she rasped. "All is gone. Evil has won. The city is dead."

"Why are you still here?" Mohamad pleaded. "This is no place for you to be."

"My time has come, sir. I am finished too. I will die here today. I know it. I am ready. My life here has been good but now I am too old to run. I cannot leave my home."

"Please, come with me," Mohamad pleaded.

"Listen," the old woman said, leaning out from her doorway and pointing into the sky.

Mohamad listened. Birdless silence, broken only by the rush of blood from his pounding heart. The Siamese cannon fire had stopped. The Burmese had surely reached the fortress from the north. Turning back to the old woman, he pleaded with her.

"Come now. We must leave immediately. I will help you."

"No," she said. "You leave. I am staying here in the only place I know. Go."

He turned to leave. "Go far from here," the old woman insisted. "Tell our story to everyone you meet. Spare no detail. The world should know how great we were and how we were slain in cold blood." At the end of the street, he turned and saw her squatting on her worn stool in the doorway of her home, the place where she had once lived and loved, and would now die. She seemed at peace with the world, ready for what would come next.

9

MORAD

"Sara, how are you?" Bob asks, pushing his chair back from his office desk.

"I'm good thanks. I didn't sleep a wink, though. I was on the internet all night trying to find some ideas. You just see the same stuff recycled over again. I've found some interesting information about Persian embassy trips to Asia. Have you ever read a book called *The Ship of Suleiman*?"

"Oh yes," Bob says. "I remember reading that in the '70s as an undergraduate, Sara, way before you were even thought of. That was probably written over a century before your document. Keep an open mind, eh?" Bob passes her a flash drive. "These are the images. They've done a nice job. Print them out if you want to but don't let them out of your sight. And don't open them on a public computer. When you see Morad, show him the documents, get his view, suss him out. If he seems reliable, we'll need to ask him to sign a non-disclosure agreement and offer him co-authorship on anything we publish. Before we let him loose."

"No problem, Bob. I'm impressed with how quickly you've whirred into action. I'm seeing Morad first thing in the morning. One small detail, though."

"Yes?"

"Morad's a woman. Professor Jaasmin Malakeh Morad."

"Whoopsie daisy. What a wonderful name." He turns back to his desk, adding over his shoulder, "Have fun. Oh, and enjoy the wine. Unoaked Chardonnay. South African. Let me know how you get on with it."

Jaasmin Morad's office could not be more different to Bob Oakhurst's den: hers is simple and gracefully furnished, with no sign of academic activity apart from a neat pile of papers on one side of a dark wooden table; no chair at the table, only low seating, upholstered in cream linen with peacock blue silk cushions. On a square coffee table sits a simple brass bowl of oranges and a polished cedar box of dates.

"Mint tea, Miss Richardson?" asks Morad, a well-dressed, fine-skinned woman, possibly in her late fifties. Sara at once falls in love with her graceful aura.

"That would be wonderful," Sara replies immediately. "Thank you." She has never liked mint tea.

They both sit and Morad speaks while preparing the tea. "I believe we have something in common, Sara. My secretary was just telling me that your middle name is Yasmin. How delightful. Where did that come from?"

"Oh, my mother chose it. I was born in Malaysia. There was a famous film maker there called Yasmin Ahmad. My mother was a bit obsessed with her."

"I see. That's so lovely, isn't it? Take some sugar with your tea, it's better that way. It's possibly stronger than you are used to."

Sara sits back and smiles. Morad continues, "You know that Dr Oakhurst has shared with me images of a document you have found. The text is Persian, of course, probably dating from the sixteenth or seventeenth century, purely on the basis of the styling. Sara, this is *very* interesting. I am hoping you have brought more for me to see?"

Sara follows Morad's advice and sweetens her tea, which she now sips from the silver-lipped glass. "Yes, here is a copy of the entire document." She hands Morad a spiral-bound folder. Morad sits back in her chair and turns the pages.

"My God," she gasps after a few moments.

"Professor Morad?"

"It's beautiful. It's so rare. So important."

"What is it?"

"Believe it or not, it's a set of recipes, Sara. They are written in Persian script… but actually, not all of them are written by the same person. Some are written later by a different hand – possibly more than one, I think. These recipes look rather like the sort of dishes you might have seen in a rich Persian household hundreds of years ago, but the ingredients seem to have changed. They're more like Asian ingredients. Here, for example…" she points at the page in front of her, "… the milk of white coconut flesh

– that's certainly not Persian. And here's something I don't even recognise."

Sara listens as Morad started to reveal the secrets of what, in 1768, a Dutch legal clerk clearly mistook for a Chinese manuscript.

"The front pages explain – I'm just roughly translating here, I'll need to spend more time on this – 'Here the reader will find instruction, carried across sea and land from one royal kitchen to another... a generous gift from God... these delicacies have been chosen by royal decree.' There's something here about a Persian kitchen in the Court of... what does that say? Siam. Sara, it says 'Siam'. Then here, 'a great fire.'"

"And the map, Professor, what do you think of that?"

Morad pauses, studies the map and realises what she is looking at. Her voice catches with emotion. "Oh, Sara, this is unbelievable. Truly remarkable. I believe this is the ancient capital of Thailand – then called Siam, of course. A great, walled city called Ayutthaya."

She traces a slender finger over the image. "An island at the junction of four great rivers. A royal island of golden temples, pagodas, palaces, wonderful ceremony. Unimaginable beauty. The Venice of ancient Asia. Persians are known to have established trade links with Siamese merchants there way before the Europeans arrived. And you, dear Sara, you clever thing – you appear to have discovered a lost link to those times."

10

A SECOND BODY

5pm. Team debrief.

DS Suwannachot speaks first. He and DC Tonpan have spent the day talking to residents of the waterfront houses north of Wat Arun, up as far as the Bangkok Noi, a branch off the main river channel. No one there, or around Thonburi rail station, has reported anything untoward. "As usual," Suwannachot adds, a look of tired resignation etched on his face from years of questioning the citizens of Bangkok, "no one ever sees or hears anything in this place."

DC Horapong and DC Jaipakdee have covered the northern bank of Bangkok Noi. No one claims to have seen anything there either, but the housing is very dense at that point and they haven't been able to finish their inspection before heading back to the team debrief.

"Thanks, Horapong, you get to go back tomorrow, first light," Kongsin smirks. "I want every lane inspected, every alleyway checked, every resident questioned, every dog turd examined. This is going to be tough work, believe me."

A young detective walks in just as Kongsin has finished speaking. She looks flustered. He holds up a hand.

"Not now, Jattawan, we're in the middle of something. Give me ten minutes, eh?"

"But sir, you need to know this now," she says. "I'm afraid it can't wait."

"What is it?"

"Another body's been recovered from the Chao Phraya." She slides an A4 photo onto the table in front of Kongsin. "Male, forties, business suit, shot in the back of the head, execution-style, sir. Face is a mess. Found under Rama IX Bridge. He's over at Pathum Wan now. Joe Yunram wants to do the autopsy before he goes home. You need to go, sir."

Kongsin raises his eyebrows and stares at the young detective. "Why the urgency, Jattawan?" Something is telling him his day is about to get a lot worse.

"Because," the DC says nervously, "because he was Naz Khan's driver, sir, that's why. There's a car waiting outside for you."

"Ah, shit." Kongsin closes his eyes, fighting the temptation to pound the desk with his clenched fist. He turns to his team. "What did I say? I told you, didn't I? This is not the sort of day you dream of. What a fine fuck this one is turning out to be." The room falls silent.

He turns to DS Suwannachot. "Right then. Before you pack in for the night, can you run a search for reports of anything unusual at all last night? I mean *anything*. Something. Raised voices, gun shots, stolen cars, burnt out cars…" He grabs his jacket and leaves the room, adding, "I'll see if I can get this guy's car details. We'll need to track that on CCTV if possible."

11

EXECUTION

Yunram's technician is already stitching the cadaver closed when Kongsin arrives at the mortuary with DC Jattawan.

"Kris, I think you have a multiple murder here, my friend. This chap is Natchapon Janjaturapan. Forty-five years old, married, two teenage kids, lived out in Bang Kapi district." He hands Kongsin a sheet of paper. "That's his address, we got it from his driver's licence. And here's his business card. He had a few in his wallet."

Executive Chauffeurs PCL
Mercedes Specialists
Mr Natchapon Janjaturapan
Contract chauffeur for Ms Naz Khan,
two Michelin-starred chef
02-2133331
info@exec-chauffeur.th

Kongsin scans the card and shakes his head. Whoever's

dumped this body has done a lousy clean-up job. Golden rule of a murder: keep the police guessing; don't help them by labelling the body. Must have been in a hurry.

"Someone will have to tell his wife, of course," Yunram says.

That irritates Kongsin. "Hey, Joe, we'll do the cop thing here, thanks, my friend. You just do the pathology and leave the big boy stuff to us while you go home for your dinner. We *have* done this before, you know."

Yunram winks at DC Jattawan. Annoying. Kongsin has been a constant source of amusement for years.

"Of course," he says. "How rude of me, Detective. Cause of death was a classic assassin's shot to the occiput; he was probably kneeling at the time, which would explain the position of the entry wound. Point blank this time, judging from residue and scorch. Bullet passed diagonally down through his head. Exit through his upper teeth, took out his nasal septum and tongue. Nasty but quick. Poor bastard. He would just about have had enough time to know what was about to happen to him. Doubly incontinent."

DC Jattawan has seen corpses before and has always considered herself to be tough cookie but tonight she is finding Yunram's matter-of-fact manner chilling. He has managed to neatly reduce the end of a human life to a few short emotionless facts. Before the evening is over, she knows she will have to witness Kongsin telling this man's wife that her future has ended.

"Time of death?"

"Hard to pinpoint. Definitely today, after 2am and probably before 6am, in my opinion."

"Same weapon?"

"All I can really say is that the damage in both bodies is of similar extent. *Could* be the same weapon. Different killings really – Khan probably saw her killer before she was shot through the face. This guy was clearly executed, so he either killed Khan and someone took a disliking to him, or he saw who killed her and had to be removed – that's my guess anyway. I can't find anything on either body that would suggest a location yet. We have some mud from his trousers but I doubt that'll lead us to a specific spot. Both bodies will be here for a while so we can always go back to them if you find anything yourselves."

Kongsin turns to DC Jattawan. "I reckon this guy probably knew too much. He'd probably seen the Khan murder, or at least knew who did it. The fact that Khan was shot in the face and this guy was executed from behind suggests that Khan died first. For once I agree with Dr Yunram here that this unfortunate guy had to be silenced before he could reveal Khan's killer. Come on, we need to get to Bang Kapi. We have a family to ruin."

Two hours later Kongsin is sitting in a car opposite Natchapon Janjaturapan's apartment, drawing heavily on a cigarette. He turns to DC Jattawan who is sitting, wet-eyed, staring ahead.

"You know," he says, "this gets shitter every time. I used to be able to switch off and just do the deed. Maybe I'm going soft but it's just not as easy as it used to be. Poor girl. Will you get the liaison team in to her for me?"

"Sure," Jattawan replies. "Sir, you were very gentle. I was very impressed. There's no easy way to break news like this. Come on, let's get back to the station and see what Suwannachot's come up with before you get some sleep." She starts the engine and pulls away, leaving the Janjaturapan family to spend their first shattered night in grief.

12

ARE YOU SITTING DOWN?

From: *Jaasmin Morad >j.morad@soas.ac.uk*
To: *Sara Richardson >s.y.richardson@london.ac.uk*
Cc: *Bob Oakhurst >r.t.oakhurst@london.ac.uk*
Date: *24.03.20 12:04*
Att: *Siam1.pdf*
Subject: First batch of translation: are you sitting down?

Dear Sara and Bob

Well, I haven't had as much fun in years! Sorry for the slight delay, I wanted to make sure I didn't miss any details. I have managed to get the first ten or so pages pretty well translated, and I must tell you, you are both in for a real treat. Of course, Sara, this has almost nothing to do with your main PhD study, but it might be worth reconsidering your future career ambitions!

At this point I think we ought to be finding a food historian of some sort to validate this translation and tell us how unique these recipes are. You know this isn't my own area of expertise – I tend to spend my time studying ancient love poetry!

In my view, this document is quite possibly the missing link between Persian cuisine and some of the 'Royal Thai' cuisine in which we find dishes that clearly have a North Indian/Middle Eastern influence, but no-one seems to know exactly where they came from. But don't quote me on that, I'm just relying on Professor Google!

Anyway, have a read and a think and maybe we should meet soon to discuss. At the moment, I haven't had time to look at the other pages (there are about ten more that are in reasonable condition and then they become quite damaged).

All the best and feel free to ask questions.

J

Jaasmin Morad

Professor of Iranian Cultural Studies
School of Oriental and African Studies

13

AT THE QUAYSIDE

Mohamad reached the quay at noon by crawling down a narrow alleyway between two merchant warehouses. He crouched low to the ground, surveying the scene around him through the haze of stinging smoke drifting across the river. Enemy soldiers were loading prisoners onto sampans and captured merchant ships. The squat brick fortress, built to defend the city against attack from the river, stood abandoned. A group of soldiers was busy tying captured women together in groups of six before pushing them, screaming, into waiting boats. Many had already been raped in front of their families while desperately attempting to flee the invading army. Their fate was now certain, but unimaginable.

Then he saw the city's children. Slain by Burmese sword and cast into the river, their tiny broken bodies now floated among the clamouring sampans.

Young Siamese men, chosen for hard labour, fought bravely against their captors as they were held face-down on the quayside, their ankles pierced through and threaded together with cords of twisted rattan. Their cries of agony joined the women's cries of despair. Mohamad panicked. Azra. The children.

Two older men sat back to back on the quayside, bound together, their heads bowed, waiting quietly as the scene raged around them as if, for them, time had briefly stopped. An agitated young soldier was standing over them shouting orders at them but they did not respond. He hauled them to their feet and pushed them over the edge of the quay into a sampan below. Neither cried out. Mohamad recognised their sad faces from the Chinese market: one, the Imperial furniture maker, the other, a potter whose glazed cooking vessels were once a favourite in the Imperial Court kitchens. Two proud men stripped of their pasts in an instant.

But Mohamad did not see Azra or his children.

He paused briefly to pray for strength, then crawled down to the quayside and slipped silently into the blood-red river, holding his goatskin bag above his head. He moved unseen along the water's edge then pushed, retching, through the floating mat of mutilated bodies to reach the sampan in which the carpenter and potter now sat. The low bamboo shelter at the stern created a narrow strip of shade where he waited, submerged to his nose, praying frantically.

In time, two other men were thrown into the boat, joined by two young Burmese soldiers with shouted orders to transport the human cargo home. They occupied themselves with freeing the sampan with a long pole and moving it through the jam of similar craft clamouring at the water's edge. Mohamad leapt into the boat while their attention was taken with untangling themselves from floating wreckage. The four bound men stared at him with wide-eyed disbelief.

"What in God's name are you doing?" hissed the carpenter.

Mohamad pleaded. "Trust me, sir. I will explain everything in time but for now, please don't make any noise!" He hid his bag under a rice sack and sat with the other men, knees drawn up to his chest, pulse hammering in his neck.

Poling the sampan across to the main river channel took the full attention of one of the soldiers while the other sat studying the captives on board. All of them were visibly terrified by the thought of their fate. Four of the men were clearly bound together in pairs but there was a fifth man, unbound. *Five?*

"Hey, Nara!" the soldier yelled up to his colleague.

"What? I'm busy here. Your turn soon, eh?"

"Did the boss say four prisoners or five?"

"Why?"

"Well, we've got five on board here. I thought we were only taking four."

"No idea. What does it matter? They'll probably all die in any case."

"Fair point. As long as *we* get home alive, I really don't care. I can't speak their language so I've no idea if we've got an extra one or not."

"Forget it. Let's just get this job done. I think it's safe to untie them; they know we'll kill them if they make a run for it. In any case, if they manage to get to the shore, they won't last five minutes."

And so the young soldier called Thiri took a long, curved blade from his belt and cut the ropes binding four of the men. He held the tip of the blade to each of the men's throats in turn.

"Try to escape and I'll kill you," he sneered.

Mr Jiang Xin, the furniture maker from the Chinese market, replied in perfect Burmese, "Young man, we are peaceful old men living peaceful lives. We have done you no wrong. What are you doing with us? Why do you speak to us like this?"

Thiri startled. "Hey, Nara! This one speaks our language!"

"Then tell him where we're going and tell him to keep his mouth shut or his head will join all the others out there." Nara pointed to the river.

Thiri spoke. "You're worth something to us, old man. Most of your fellow citizens are good for nothing but whoring, hard labour or Hell. But you're all different, see? You're useful to us. We're taking you 'artisans' back to work for our own King. We *own* you now." He added, "And how did you come to speak our language, old man?"

Jiang Xin replied, "This isn't the first time your armies have attacked us, young soldier. I'm a tradesman. I'm Chinese. It pays to know who's your enemy and who's your customer. If you want to trade with the Burmese, you have to speak their tongue."

"Ha! And who am I, old man? Enemy or customer?"

"You and your kind have always been, and will always be, my enemy," Jiang Xin explained calmly. "You are just another obedient young dog in a pack of greedy, ignorant dogs."

Soldier Thiri didn't push his blade into Jiang's neck as his instinct told him. Instead, he tightened his fist and struck him mid-face, crushing his nose and knocking him backwards into Mohamad.

"And we dogs have pissed on your nation once more." He barked and Nara howled, mocking their captives.

14

SUWANNACHOT

"Where do you want me to start, boss? Last night, this proud and peaceful city reported over one thousand incidents on the phone helpline and logged two thousand five hundred online notifications." Suwannachot rips the wrapper off the end of a chocolate bar and bites off a chunk. "But if I restrict it to incidents from the west bank," he mumbles, "we are only left with a thousand. And if I search 'gunshot' I get fifteen reports clustered in five different sites."

"And? What's the punchline, DS Suwannachot? The suspense is literally pissing me off here."

"Sorry, sir. Interestingly, there are two reports of shouting and maybe a gunshot from a residential block called Riverview Mansions, just south of Rama VIII Bridge at 2am."

"Interesting precisely because…?"

"Precisely because, sir, there were a couple of gunshot reports around Khlong Dusit at 4am." Seeing Kongsin's blank expression, Suwannachot adds, "Khlong Dusit is only a few hundred metres downstream from Riverview Mansions. It's a bit of a long shot – excuse the pun, sir – but the other reports are scattered all over the city and don't seem to fit any pattern. Do we have a time of death for Khan's driver?"

"Between 2am and 6am, as it happens. Nice work, detective, you may have just earned yourself a beer. I'll let you know what we find. Go get some rest now, eh?"

15

CHAMPAGNE

From: *Sara Richardson >s.y.richardson@london.ac.uk*
To: *Jaasmin Morad >j.morad@soas.ac.uk*
Cc: *Bob Oakhurst >r.t.oakhurst@london.ac.uk*
Date: *24.03.20 14:22*
Att:
Subject: Re: First batch of translation: are you sitting down?

OMG!

Professor this is unbelievable! I don't even know where to begin – although maybe the kitchen would be a good place!! Thank you so much for what you have done so far. I need time to get my head around this. I'll speak to Bob and we'll get some dates to you ASAP for a meeting.

    Sara x

From: *Bob Oakhurst >r.t.oakhurst@london.ac.uk*

To: *Sara Richardson >s.y.richardson@london.ac.uk*

Cc:

Date: *24.03.20 14:30*

Att:

Subject: Re: First batch of translation: are you sitting down?

Sara

I think this is going to turn out to be a very significant discovery. Do not show this translation to anyone. We need to identify a food historian and speak to the press officer. I'm in my office at the moment – if you pick this message up before 5pm, why don't you pop over and we'll draw up a battle plan. I know a nice little wine bar in Fitzrovia where we can hide from the rest of the world!

Well done, you clever thing. This is a career-maker. I can see lecture tours and publications on the back of this one!

See you later.

RTO

R T Oakhurst MA(Oxon) DPhil FRS

Chief Curator, African and Asian Archives
British Library

Ordinarily, the short walk from the School of Oriental and African Studies to the British Library would be full of familiar distractions – the elegant Georgian terraces with their cast-iron balconies, the maple trees of Tavistock Square on the point of budburst, the old bow-fronted shop fronts of Woburn Walk – but today Sara is walking quickly, head down, unaware of the world around her. She is numb with excitement, more so than at any time in her life so far. Almost without pausing to breathe, she crosses Euston Road, marches across the plaza in front of the library, past Paolozzi's great bronze of Isaac Newton, between the security guards, across the foyer to the elevators, up to the second floor and past Mary to Bob Oakhurst's office.

She stands, breathless, looking at Oakhurst's back.

"Ah, Sara. Do come in. Professor Jaasmin has just been on the phone, actually. She's quite beside herself, I don't quite know what to say. This is a new one on me, Sara. No bargain booze tonight, my dear, this is one of those champagne moments!"

16

CHAO PHRAYA

Nara finally steered the sampan into the Chao Phraya River. They drifted past the abandoned Dutch compound, once busy with trading vessels and the chatter of foreign tongues, the setting sun silhouetting temple spires against a deep tangerine canvas streaked with towering columns of black smoke. No one spoke. Only the fading, anguished cries from the quayside punctured the silence.

That evening, the Burmese sat eating fruit while the boat floated slowly downstream. They slept in shifts, one always watching the prisoners, who sat engulfed in silent torment. By dawn, the dark palm trees of Koh Rien Island slowly pierced through the dense morning river mist. From the island's mud banks rose jagged lines of timber posts – the ribs of rotting trading junks, grounded years before on their way upriver, now a line of decaying teeth, waiting to snag the unwary. Thiri steered towards the riverbank where a small, worn pier at the water's edge provided a mooring point in a thicket of fan palms. Ayutthaya was still visible on the horizon, the grey pre-dawn sky smeared with the colour of fire.

There was no food or water on board, apart from uncooked rice. Thiri spoke to Jiang Xin. "Get out and stretch. Take the others with you. If you find food, help yourselves and bring some back to the boat. Stay close by. Do as I say, and we'll all be fine. Do you hear?"

Jiang Xin nodded and spoke to the other men. One by one, they leapt from the sampan and disappeared into the thick vegetation. A little distance from the river was a long-deserted temple compound, now largely reclaimed by the forest. The five men stood there in silence, watched by macaques hiding in the shade and cranes circling slowly on the warming air above them. Mohamad was the first to speak.

"Sirs, please allow me to introduce myself. My name is Mirkazemi. Mohamad Mirkazemi. I am not an artisan like you. I was not captured by these people. I escaped, but without my family. I sent my wife and children to the quay ahead of me yesterday morning. Now I have no idea where they are."

Jiang Xin spoke next. "You are fortunate to have survived, my friend. I am Jiang Xin. I watched my own wife being tied up and thrown into a junk with her mother and our fourteen-year-old daughter. I was powerless to do anything. I could not help them. By now they must be dead. These pigs will pay for this, however long it takes."

Another spoke. "I am Chi She. I have a shop in the Chinese market. I make pots. Clay pots."

"I know your shop well," said Mohamad, recognising Mr Chi's face. "I bought many pots from you over the years."

"Yes, of course, Mr Mirkazemi. I should have recognised your face before now. My family fled like yours. I have lost them too. My wife. My son…"

Jiang Xin placed an arm around him. "Mr Chi," he said, "we need to be strong. We must survive this. One day we will be reunited with our families, in this life or the next." He looked up through bloodshot eyes. "But for now, we must all try to stay alive."

Mohamad remembered the old woman in the doorway of her shop. "We need to tell the world what happened to our city."

So far, the two other men had been silent. The younger spoke first. "I am Bai. Bai Dong. This is my father, Bai Jian. We tried to escape through the Chinese Gate with our family. We always kept a boat on the canal near our home. We nearly made it. But we were caught on the river…"

His father continued, "These peasants took our women from us, ran our children through with their swords, threw their tiny bodies into the river. We saw it all."

Jiang Xin broke the angry silence that followed. "Listen to me," he said. "We have to be strong. Let's take some of this fruit," he pointed to orange trees and wild pineapples still growing in the temple compound, "and some of the coconuts over here. We should go back to the boat now or the soldiers will come looking for us."

By now, the sun was climbing above the trees and the river mist had cleared. As the men sat in the shade at the back of the sampan eating their fruit and drinking water from the coconuts, they realised with growing horror that the mats of debris floating silently past their mooring place were not the usual tangles of vegetation but were fragments of people. Their own townsfolk. Maybe their own families. A steady, relentless stream of death.

Bai Dong looked up at the soldiers. "You bastards!" he screamed at them. "Look at what you have done! Look at our dead! Look at them! I'll see that you are reborn in Hell for this!" He lunged at Thiri, roaring with fury, throwing the sampan violently as he knocked him across the face with a huge, tight fist. Jiang Xin jumped on Bai Dong's back, pleading for him to stop.

"What are you saying to me, arsehole?" Thiri replied, his lip split and bleeding. He snatched the knife from his belt.

Jiang Xin pleaded frantically, placing himself between Bai Dong and Thiri. "He's angry, can't you see? Can't you see our people? Can't you understand? Are you *really* that heartless? We have all lost our families and yet here we sit, eating fruit as if nothing happened, while bits of our wives and children are floating by. What do you *seriously* expect us to do?"

Thiri snarled back, "And do you *seriously* think we give a shit, old man? Do you think we want to be here? Those bodies are just vermin. You're all vermin. You should all have been killed."

Nara grabbed the knife from Thiri's hand. "Don't. Don't even think about it," he said. "We have to keep them alive."

Thiri held a cloth to his torn lip. "You can tell your fat friend I'll slice his heart out if he tries that again."

Jiang Xin translated. "He's serious. Sit down, will you? Go to the back of the boat." Turning to face the other men, he warned, "If we are to survive, we need to be calm. The other soldier seems to be more sensible. Let's keep him on our side."

Nara untied the sampan and pushed it from the riverbank into the current. Soon they were drifting southwards again and as they passed abandoned orchards and dense stands of palm trees, Mohamad watched the last spires of his beloved city slip behind the horizon forever. No word was spoken that long afternoon. The Burmese soldiers sat at the bow, eyes fixed on their five captives. No one looked into the river. Only the slap of water against the hull or the screech of monkeys on the riverbank broke the heavy mood. As the setting sun bathed flooded rice fields with copper light, Thiri manoeuvred the sampan to the river's edge, where several collapsing bamboo huts stood on stilts.

"We'll stay here tonight. At dawn, you will go ashore again to find food and water," Nara ordered. He lit a small oil lamp and placed it on a rice sack. He and Thiri spent the evening joking and laughing while they ate the remaining fruit in front of their captives. Bai Dong lay furthest from them, on his side, facing away from the others. His father placed one hand on his shoulder and sat at his back, motionless, staring into the distance. Jiang Xin, Chi She and Mohamad lay deep in their thoughts, sleeping fitfully, haunted.

At dawn-break, the men were kicked awake by Thiri, with the exception of Bai Dong, who he left alone. Four of them jumped ashore, leaving Bai Dong behind, still lying on his side.

"Is he OK?" Chi She asked Bai Jian.

"Leave him for a while. He is mourning his family.

He'll come round sooner or later. No man should ever see what he saw."

The four men walked from the sampan along a ridge raised between paddy fields. In time, they came to a small group of dwellings. Jiang Xin called out, but no one replied. Mohamad surveyed the nearest house.

"Nothing here," he reported. "Looks like there was a struggle." The men found a similar scene in the other houses. "There's good clean water though."

In one field they found chickens and managed to catch two of them. In another, they found unharvested beans and nuts. They retraced their steps through the village, pausing for a while to sit in the shade of areca palms while enjoying a snatched moment of freedom. They discussed the possibility of escape but knew they would almost certainly be tracked down and killed if they tried. They walked in silence back to captivity.

17

GUN SHOTS

Thursday 17ᵗʰ August, 6am

Chakrawat Police Station incident room has taken on a different air this morning. Kongsin, fortified as usual by black Vietnamese Robusta from the street vendor outside, is standing in front of a large whiteboard on which DS Suwannachot has fixed images of the two bodies and a large map showing the northern shore of Bangkok Noi, running north as far as the Rama VIII Bridge.

Kongsin shouts above the morning chatter. "Come on, settle down, will you? Today's a big day. I need you all on top form and working at high speed. Let's look at the facts. Fact one: we know that Khan was killed by a gunshot to the face in the early hours of Wednesday 16ᵗʰ August. Fact two: her body was then dumped in the Chao Phraya, where it got snagged on the Khun Mae Pueak ferry pier. Worshippers leaving Wat Arun found her at 6.45am. Fact three: we haven't got a lead on who did this and what he used to kill her. I say 'he' because it usually is. Fact four: Janjaturapan was killed – very deliberately by the looks of it – by a shot to the back of the head some time later but probably before 6am. Fact five: his body was retrieved from the Chao Phraya at 17.30 hours yesterday. Fact six: fuck knows who did this, but it's tempting to assume it's the same person that shot Khan.

"Our resident sleuth DS Suwannachot has identified a cluster of gunshot reports in this area." He points to the map with his pen. "The first reports from around 2.10am were dialled in from residents in Riverview Mansions. Looks like a nice, sleepy sort of place; not the kind of residents who usually go around killing each other. The second cluster of reports was from around 4am, a bit further downstream at Khlong Dusit, just to the north of where Bangkok Noi meets the Chao Phraya."

DC Horapong speaks next. "DC Jaipakdee and I were in that area yesterday, boss. Can I ask why these reports weren't followed up by Royal Thai Police when they were called in last night?"

"Your guess is as good as mine, DC Horapong, but thankfully we have DS Suwannachot's immense brain on our side."

Across the table Suwannachot is grazing on a jumbo tub of peanuts, smiling broadly and nodding in agreement with Kongsin's assessment.

"So, get out there again. Let DS Suwannachot know the moment you think you have something; we'll need forensics on site without delay. I don't have to remind you we are treating this as a high-profile double murder, and we need to find the killer immediately. I have a press conference booked for 9am. I'll come over after that. Let's get this nailed, people. Questions?"

Horapong said, "Boss, the weather forecast for today is shit. If there's any physical evidence outside, we'd better focus a bigger team on Khlong Dusit just in case."

"Good point. Take DC Jaipakdee, Jattawan and Tonpan. DS Suwannachot, will you go and find the security officers at Riverview Mansions?"

"Sure," Suwannachot says. "And, boss?"

"Yes?"

"I ran a further check last night. There were ten reports of vehicle fires yesterday between 7am and 7pm. One of them was a Mercedes on fire in an old industrial unit out on the Ekkachai Road. Janjaturapan drove a Mercedes, sir."

"OK, get uniform to secure the scene. Can we get a forensics team over there straight away? Keep me informed, eh?"

Kongsin downs the dregs of his coffee, gives a thumbs-up to Suwannachot and leaves the office to brief Captain Chainarong before facing the press.

18

MURDER

Chi She was the first to arrive at the water's edge.

Bai Dong was standing waist-deep in the river, holding Thiri's limp, headless body across his forearms. In one clenched hand he held the soldier's own knife.

Jiang Xin arrived next, followed by Bai Dong's father, then Mohamad. They stood motionless, shocked, trying to make sense of the scene before them. Bai Jian sank to his knees and wailed. "My son! My son! What have you done?"

Bai Dong shouted his reply from somewhere deep inside his body, his voice spittle-flecked and raw. "We are free men now, father. The dogs are dead." He rolled Thiri's body into the current and signalled to the sampan. Nara's body was arched over the bow, his throat cut deeply by Thiri's blade. Dark blood slicked down the side of the sampan, pooling on the muddy riverbank.

"Their souls will suffer for eternity for what they have done to us," Bai Dong raged. He hurled the knife into the middle of the river, casually rinsed his bloody hands and arms and waded back to the bank. His father, still kneeling, looked up at his son, unable to comprehend the scene.

Chi She was the first to move. "Come," he urged the others, clutching Mohamad's arm and pulling him in the direction of the boat. "Leave them to it. We need to get rid of this body quickly before someone sees us." Mohamad climbed quickly on board and lifted Nara's legs, tipping him over the side. The dead soldier slapped heavily into the bloody river mud. Jiang Xin and Chi She dragged him to the water's edge and pushed him in. Nara's corpse drifted away downstream, just one body among countless other murdered souls.

No words were exchanged as the three men scooped up river water to wash Nara's blood from the sampan. Nearby, Bai Dong sat beside his father, gazing out at the river, breathing deeply through flared nostrils, heart pounding.

Bai Jian spoke calmly. "My son, what you have done to these men is very wrong. But what their kind has done to ours is a much greater wrong than this. In time you will face your punishment as a man before God, but it is not my place to punish you now. My love does not end here." He placed a thin hand on his son's back. "Come now. We should leave immediately. These lands are no longer ours. We'll be caught and killed if we stay here, it's too dangerous."

On board the sampan, everyone knew instinctively what they needed to do. The brutal deaths of the two young men called Thiri and Nara were never discussed – not then, nor at any time over the coming days as they continued downriver. It was as if the Divine River had washed away a great evil without leaving a trace. Secretly, each man felt that the slaughter of these two soldiers was small reparation for the sins of their army. Secretly, each man wished he had killed them with his own hands.

Mohamad pushed the sampan from the river's edge, past the stilted houses and on towards uncertainty.

19

JENNY PULMAN

From: *Jenny Pulman >jenny.pulman@food.history.net*
To: *Jaasmin Morad >j.morad@soas.ac.uk*
Cc: *Bob Oakhurst; Sara Richardson*
Date: *26.03.20 16.05*
Att:
Subject: Your manuscript

Dear all

Thanks for asking my opinion on your manuscript. I hope you got my signed Confidentiality Agreement; actually, I think that's a really good idea and in this particular case I think you are going to need to control the release of this information.

You might be aware that although I describe myself as a food historian, my particular interest is in Ancient Egypt and the Levant rather than Persia. However, I have done some reading, and I can see that there is a great deal of controversy about how the 'Muslim' cooking style got into

Thai cuisine. There is a dish called 'Massaman curry', for example, which seems to have generated more debate than most other dishes I can think of (except for Yorkshire pudding...).

I think you'd have to go outside the UK for a definitive opinion but I happen to know a chap called Jatupol Bamrung based in Bangkok. I met him many years ago at a conference and have stayed in touch ever since. He's Professor of Cultural History at one of the universities over there. His work is well respected and I think he's the man for the job. I can introduce you to him if you are happy for me to do that.

I agree with you that if this manuscript is the real deal, it seems to be an important piece of the jigsaw puzzle and gives wonderful insight into how a cuisine evolves with cultural exchange.

Let me know. Exciting!

Jen

Dr Jenny Pulman
Freelance Food Historian

20

STORIES

The five men soon established a cautious daily pattern to avoid being seen. From dawn to mid-morning, they drifted downstream, remaining as close to the eastern bank as possible. As noon approached, they would find a sheltered place to moor the sampan, shielded from view by palm branches. One of them would act as sentry while the others slept as best they could in the midday heat. In the late afternoon, they would explore the area close to their mooring spot, collecting food and fresh water where possible, returning while the sun was low in the sky to continue their journey. When night fell and the river turned to swirling ink, they would once again find a place to stop, then eat. It was during these secret evening meals that they finally started to relax a little and share their stories.

On the fourth night, after a meal of coconut flesh and over-ripe guavas, Mohamad spoke. "Jiang Xin. Will you tell us about your journey? How did you come to be in Ayutthaya?"

The eldest of the group smiled, his soft, lined face and brown eyes faintly lit by the oil lamp. "Well, there's nothing else to talk about, I suppose," he began. "I wasn't born in Siam, of course. I arrived with my father in 1730 when I was just ten years old – that tells you how ancient I really am. I was born in China in a small village in Shandong province. My father worked in the local town as a general trader, selling whatever he could – fruit and vegetables mostly. When business was good and he had money in his pocket, he used to transport wine and animal skins overland to Qingdao. There, he would charter a junk to take his goods by sea to Canton, where he could exchange them for cloth."

The other men listened in silence, absorbed.

"He made his fortune, but that was never enough for him. He set his eyes on a greater prize after speaking to traders in Canton from far-away places like India, Sri Lanka and Japan. In the markets there, he saw every colour of man, heard every spoken tongue. He used to tell me about the goods on sale there: Malayan spices, silks from India, precious metals from all over China, copper from Japan, tin from Siam, incense, paper, rice… just about everything you could ever wish for."

The oil lamp dimmed, spluttered and faded, throwing the group into perfect darkness.

"Carry on, Mr Jiang," Mohamad urged.

"The market everyone wanted to get into was the legendary Imperial City of Ayutthaya. Everyone who had been there told stories of golden spires, great elephant pageants, untold treasures and thriving market trade with merchants who travelled by sea all the way from Europe.

We'd never seen a white-skinned man before. The place was full of them, by all accounts!

"Father being Father, he moved us to Ayutthaya to establish an importation company. We came by sea, first to Canton, where father loaded a junk with as much as it could safely carry, and when the winds were right, we set off across the South China Sea. It took over two months to reach Siam. The weather was terrible. My mother and sister cried for a week. We puked for most of the time! There was nothing for us to do, the conditions were cramped and the food was awful. I don't think my mother ever really recovered.

"I remember the journey up this very river. All of our goods had to be transferred from our junk to smaller boats. I remember being bitten alive by flies where the river is wide and slow, the endless turns to the left and right, but then," he paused as if he was reliving the journey, "then the magical countryside, the orchards, the pure clean air and, best of all, our first sighting of Ayutthaya." He smiled to himself. "I remember seeing a beautiful monastery on the east bank of the river, then, just visible in the distance, the tips of the temple spires inside the city itself. Real gold, glinting in the sun. I have never forgotten that moment…"

Jiang Xin stopped. Remembering his arrival as an excited child made his current situation feel so much worse.

"You know?" he said softly in the darkness. "I think I'll leave it there. It's too sad for me to carry on. I'll tell you more another day."

The men woke early, cast off and made good progress hidden within a cloak of heavy mist, accompanied by the sound of egrets' wings slapping on the surface of the river as they took flight ahead of the sampan. Just past the old Customs House, where chains once ran from bank to bank to control the passage of vessels sailing northwards, the river took a long meander to the west, and by mid-morning they had drawn level with the monastery that Jiang Xin had mentioned the previous evening.

"Look, Jiang Xin," beckoned Chi She. "Wat Phai Lom."

"Ah!" he gasped, shaking his head. "Is it really so?"

"Come, let's stop to pray," Bai Jian urged.

The temple stood in silence, enveloped by the forest. A pair of storks stood haughtily by the water's edge, inspecting the men as they tied up their vessel. The Chinese men walked cautiously into the temple grounds. No one greeted them. The temple doors stood open. Inside, a large gilded bronze figure of the Buddha reclined peacefully in a hall decorated with flaking paintings of his life. No incense burned at the altar. No offerings had been left for many months. The men spent a long while sitting in silence in the prayer hall with their thoughts.

Bai Jian asked for leniency from the Lord Buddha in deciding his son's eventual fate. Bai Dong asked for the souls of the murdered Burmese soldiers to be cast into eternal flame. Jiang Xin thought with great love about his parents and sister all those years ago as they arrived in their new paradise, and his wife and children now, whose whereabouts and fate he would never know. Chi She, who had never married, simply thought about his neighbours in the narrow lane where he spent his life; the noise, laughter, tragedy, toil, now just echoing memories.

Back at the sampan, Mohamad also prayed before checking on his treasured possessions, rewrapping them in their embroidered cloth and replacing them under the rice sack. When the men returned to the boat, carrying water and berries picked from temple bushes, he was dozing quietly in the morning sun, thinking about his children.

"Come on, let's get this place covered up," Bai Jian hissed. For the next few hours they hid under their palm leaf shelter, before continuing their slow passage past deserted rice fields. For a while, the river widened and slowed before they reached a tributary on the eastern bank where they spent the night.

After supper they sat under a broad fig tree, watching the light fade. As the evening chorus of frogs whirred around them, Chi She opened the evening's conversation.

"Tomorrow we should visit Sam Khok. I have heard of it but never seen it. We might find something more interesting to eat."

"It is a very ancient and holy place," Jiang Xin said, adding, "I wonder what the Burmese have done to it. We'll need to be very careful."

"My father stopped there on his journey up the Chao Phraya," Chi She continued. "For many years he ran a pottery studio back home in Suzhou, like his own father and his grandfather before him. They were famous in the district for making cooking pots, which he sold from floating shops on Suzhou's canals. When he heard about

Ayutthaya, he was only twenty-five years old, unmarried, both parents dead. I think he was looking for a new challenge, so he left China. Just like that. He joined a merchant ship and found his way to Siam. I think a lot of young men did that in those days.

"My father initially settled across the river from Ayutthaya near the Putthai Sawan monastery. He met my mother there. After they married, they were granted permission to live within the city walls and he set up a new studio just behind the Diamond Fortress." Chi She paused as vivid memories from his childhood flooded back. "I grew up completely surrounded by clay pots! In a way, I had no choice but to take up the family business, but I enjoyed every minute. Everything was going so well. And now it has all come to an end. For now, at least." Chi She stopped and bowed his head.

Bai Jian broke the silence that followed. "Mr Jiang, will you tell us what happened to you? You left us in suspense last night!"

Jiang Xin then explained how he grew up in an old courtyard house on the main street through the Chinese market with his parents, two brothers and three sisters. Next door there lived an old master craftsman from the ancient city of Wuxi on the shores of Lake Taihu. When Jiang Xin was twelve years old he became an apprentice, learning how to make furniture without glue or nails and how to carve hard woods into fantastical dragons and geometric shapes. Their workshop made ornate furniture, which proved very popular with the Imperial Court. Over the years, Jiang Xin and his master had become well-known throughout the city. He bought the old master's share of the business when he died and was in the process of handing it over to his own son when the Burmese attacked. Now, his future had been destroyed. He sobbed openly as he described how he had cradled his son in his arms as his life bled from him onto the quayside.

Still blackness closed in on the sampan. Nothing more was said that night.

BANGKOK HERALD

Khan murder: police seek double killer.

Early yesterday we learned of the death of Nazia Khan, celebrity chef and owner of two Michelin-starred Restaurant Khan, the flagship of Bangkok's international culinary scene. But there's a new twist in this tale: her faithful driver of many years, Mr Natchapon Janjaturapan of Executive Chauffeurs PCL, was also found late yesterday afternoon by bargemen working under Rama IX Bridge, shot in the head.

In a statement given this morning by Detective Inspector Kris Kongsin, we learned that both Khan and Janjaturapan appear to have been murdered using the same weapon and their deaths are assumed to be linked. Detectives are currently deployed at several sites on the west bank of the Chao Phraya.

It is of course no secret that Ms Khan had her favourites and her enemies. We tracked down a sous chef from her kitchen at Restaurant Khan, who chose to remain anonymous. She told us: "She was a formidable boss, often very critical and prone to violent rages. It was really terrifying working in her kitchen sometimes. I've seen her reduce the toughest chefs to jelly. Over the two years I worked for her, I saw many good people leave. It's sad to know she's dead, she was a great talent, but there will be many people out there who won't be sorry to see her go."

So, did Khan finally get her comeuppance? Did she push someone too far? If so, did her driver witness her murder? In this fast-paced investigation, Bangkok Herald will keep you up to date.

Thursday 17th August 2020 09.30

21

A VERY EXCITING DISCOVERY

From: *Jatupol Bamrung >JB03@chula.ac.th*
To: *Jenny Pulman >jenny.pulman@food.history.net*
Cc: *Bob Oakhurst; Sarah Richardson*
Date: *26.03.20 05.20*
Att:
Subject: Manuscript

Dear Jenny et al

Thank you for sending me the first translated pages of your Persian manuscript. I feel privileged to have seen this. You have my assurance that I will treat it with the utmost confidence. I think this is a very exciting discovery – here in Thailand it will almost certainly 'rock the boat'! It clearly shows a link between a lineage of Persian cooks working in the Royal Palace in Ayutthaya, their original Persian cuisine and the changes they needed to introduce in order to adapt their cuisine to the Siamese Royal Court. It proves – in my mind at least – that some of our favourite dishes have a traceable Persian origin. No more debate! Of course, that's not going to please everyone…

I have one question: how do you know that this is a genuine manuscript contemporaneous with the Ayutthaya period? Although it was found in a dated archive, can you guarantee its provenance? Is there a way of dating it more accurately? If you can pin it right down then I think you have a story that will capture the Thai people's imagination. Ayutthaya history is very popular here, as you can imagine, but there is always a lot of fake news.

At the moment I am going to stay quiet on this but if I can help in any way, please let me know. I presume you are planning to publish this? If so, please consider me as a co-author, I would love to write some context for you.

All the best

Jatupol

Prof Dr Jatupol Bamrung

History Department
King Rama IX University
Bangkok, Thailand

22

SAM KHOK

Bai Dong managed to manoeuvre the sampan across the river to reach Sam Khok. Over a century before, the Mon people, expelled from their homeland of Burma by their Emperor, had been allowed to settle in the small villages dotted around the Chao Phraya Valley. They brought music and dance and, in Sam Khok, established a thriving pottery industry, as Chi She's father had discovered when he had travelled this way forty years before.

A number of narrow canals led from the river into the village. Arranged along each channel were smart bamboo houses, some extending out over the water on stilts with fishing nets held out on drying poles. Behind many of these homes were gardens, once planted with vegetables and fruit trees but now neglected and already overgrown in the tropical heat. Beyond the gardens rose the ornate gilded gables of temple buildings. No human voice could be heard, no dog bark or cock crow.

"There are no boats here," Bai Jian said. "There should

be boats. People made a living from the river here. Look." He pointed at a heaped net on the ground in which long-dead silver-scaled fish and transparent river prawns had become snagged. "They didn't even have time to sort the catch. It's as if they dropped everything and ran." Bai Jian and Bai Dong stayed with the sampan while the others wandered into the village.

Mohamad tried to imagine what had happened to the villagers. Hearing footsteps behind him, he turned, expecting to see one of his comrades. Instead, an old man dressed simply in a faded monk's robe walked towards him with outstretched hands.

"Welcome, my friend!" he beamed. "You are one of the men from the boat that arrived just now?"

"I am, sir." Mohamad held the monk's hands in his. "Where is everyone, may I ask?"

"They have all gone, my son. They fled many weeks ago to escape the army that passed through here on its way to Ayutthaya. Men, women, children; many left with nothing but their clothes and a parcel of food. Fishermen's catches were left to rot in the sun. Farmers had to leave their crops to spoil in the fields. Animals had to fend for themselves. Most have perished or now roam freely in the countryside. The villagers who chose to stay were taken by the army. I was left here to tend the temples. You are the first people I have seen for many weeks."

"We were spared death at Ayutthaya. Like you, we have seen terrible things, sir, terrible things. But we have our lives and we now seek our freedom."

"I am sure you are hungry. Do you have food?" asked the holy man.

"We came here hoping we would find some. So far, no luck."

"I will prepare food for you. Go, find your friends and come back to this spot."

Mohamad returned to the sampan where Bai Jian and Bai Dong were sitting at the edge of the canal, talking. "The Burmese got here first, weeks ago," he explained. "I just met a monk at a temple nearby. He will give us food. Have you seen Mr Jiang and Mr Chi?"

"They're still sniffing around, looking for anything they can carry."

"Thank you, Dong. Come, help me find them and I will take you to meet my new friend."

The monk led the group past cold, silent kilns and deserted streets to a small enclosure beside the river. There, he prepared a simple meal of rice, pumpkin and dried shrimp, which he blessed with burning incense and offered to his visitors. They ate well in the company of their venerable host and afterwards spoke at length of their ordeals while they sipped hot tea together. In the early afternoon they bade the monk farewell, thanked him for his generosity and, with his blessing, returned to their boat, stopping to search houses and gardens for anything they might use. By the time they reached the sampan, they had collected fishing nets, tea, pumpkins, ginger, peppercorns, dried fish and salt, all of which was carefully stowed before they hid for the rest of the afternoon.

Spirits were high on board as the men from Ayutthaya

continued their journey close to the western riverbank until darkness made progress impossible. That night they ate briefly and, for the first time since leaving their beloved city, all of them slept without being interrupted by torment.

At dawn, Chi She cast a net out into the river and hauled in a catch of tiny fish, which he cooked quickly on the riverbank before the smoke from his campfire could be noticed. The men washed quietly at the cool water's edge before enjoying their breakfast together. Chi She had also boiled water for tea, which tasted good and reminded them of home. Surrounded by the quiet sounds of the river, all was calm.

The men pressed on after stamping out their fire and grinding its ashes into the riverbank, moving swiftly on a full current as the river wound to and fro for mile after mile. The mist persisted for longer than usual that morning, lingering in palm groves, drifting over the eddying water. They rested in shade at a fork in the river while the sun cleared the last of the mist. There, they debated the best onward route. Almost directly ahead of them lay the entrance to a canal, cut many years before to shorten the journey upstream taken by trading vessels. To the west was the wide entrance to an ancient, lushly forested meander of the Chao Phraya River; this, they decided, would reduce the chance of them being seen.

23

RIVERSIDE MANSIONS

Thursday 17ᵗʰ August, 8.30am

Suwannachot arrives at Riverside Mansions just after the night shift guard has left for the day. The day guard is sitting in his office, fiddling with the multi-screen system before settling into another tedious day. Something isn't quite right.

"Does anything seem out of order, mate?" Suwannachot flashes his ID and introduces himself. "I'm investigating reports of possible gunshots here last night." The guard nods and points at the two blank screens in front of him.

"Does that usually happen?" Suwannachot asks.

"No, it's normally a very reliable system, sir." The guard looks confused. "It wasn't reported though," he mumbles, flicking through the last two pages of the incident log. He calls up camera footage from the previous night. At 2.13am the video feed from the elevator plaza on floor ten went blank.

Floor ten. One of the gunshot reports was dialled in from the tenth floor, Suwannachot recalls.

Scrolling forward, the entrance foyer image also went blank, at 2.16am. Suwannachot's pulse quickens. "Can you take me to these cameras please, mate?" he asks.

The foyer camera is hanging by a cluster of coloured wires. Someone has taken a swing at it, cracking its lens and dislodging it from the ceiling. Same up on the tenth floor. Suwannachot looks around. Nothing unusual. The elevator doors open and a young couple walks past, giggling. Suwannachot notices something on the edge of the open door. He knows instinctively what he is looking at.

"I need to you to inactivate the elevator immediately please, sir. Is there any outside security coverage?"

"No, not ours. No street cameras around here either. It's a quiet neighbourhood. Nothing ever happens round here. Sometimes I wonder why we bother with security."

"For days like this, my friend. Could you get me the footage from those two cameras up to the moment they lost signal? On a flash drive. Last twenty-four hours. As soon as possible."

8.55am

Kongsin's cell phone is ringing. Suwannachot's number. He answers.

"Boss, I think we have something here."

"Speak to me, big man."

"Riverside Mansions. Gunshot reported last night but not investigated, remember? Two internal security cameras smashed out of action. Not noticed by the guard on duty, so not reported."

Kongsin rants about security guards.

"I know, boss, I know. Listen, there's blood on the elevator door at floor ten. There are eight apartments on this floor. I'm starting at 1001 and working along. Let me know when you're here."

"No you fucking don't. You'll wait for me, OK? The killer might still be up there for all you know. I'm leaving now." He takes a pistol and a couple of ammo clips from his desk drawer, loads and calls for a squad car.

Kongsin arrives at 9.10am. Suwannachot has already mobilised uniformed officers, the apartment block is cordoned off and armed guards are glowering in the foyer, H&K carbines pointing at the floor. By 9.15, Chainarong has sanctioned an immediate on-site forensics team. Up on floor ten, Suwannachot has already spoken to elderly residents in 1001 and 1002 but neither has heard anything, and in any case, they've been asleep in bed.

"Nothing yet, boss," he sighs as Kongsin wheezes out of the stairs.

"Jesus, man, I thought I told you to wait until I was here? There are no bonus points for getting a bullet in the head, you idiot. Forensics will be here soon. Let's do the rest together."

In 1003, a woman, late fifties, clearly hungover, spends a long while trying to explain that she hasn't heard anything – but to be fair, she has been busy in bed with her young boyfriend so isn't surprised by the possibility that she may have missed something.

Kongsin winces as she closed the door. "*Really*?"

"Pretty impressed she's still got it in her, boss."

"Doesn't make it right, though."

"You're just jealous."

Kongsin smirks. Maybe he is. It's been a long time.

The old couple in apartment 1004 called the local police station in the early hours of the morning, having been woken by what they claimed was a single gunshot followed by shouting. They didn't see anything and were too frightened to open their front door or step out onto their balcony. Their call was logged but no one from TRP had been to investigate.

1005 gives no response. Kongsin stands back from the door and examines the frame. Nothing.

Suwannachot is crouching halfway between 1005 and the elevator. He dabs a finger at a wet spot on the floor and lifts it towards Kongsin. Blood.

Kongsin unclips his pistol and flicks the safety catch off. Motioning to Suwannachot to stand behind him, he turns to face apartment 1005. He hammers on the door. No reply. Suwannachot, probably twice the size of Kongsin, moves to the front and heaves his left shoulder against the door.

24

A MOST RARE AND EXQUISITE FRAGMENT

At some point during the long, sweltering afternoon, Mohamad turned to Bai Jian and reminded him that he had not yet revealed his own story.

"Nor have you, Mr Mirkazemi, mystery man," Bai Jian replied, and the group listened to each in turn as they told their life stories.

Bai Jian described how he had arrived from Shanghai in 1752 at the age of thirty. There, he had studied lacquer painting under the watchful tuition of the Great Master Zhu Wei and had perfected the use of gold leaf decoration. So rare and desired were his skills that he was given a vacant studio shop within the city walls by Ayutthaya officials, and before long he met his close neighbour, Jiang Xin, who could supply him with simple wooden boxes and cabinets to be transformed into black or red lacquerware pieces. Bai Jian became well-known for his gilded decorations of fish and birds, and soon also became a favourite of the Imperial Household. He regaled the group with memories of the Chinese market in full swing, when shops groaned with goods and foreign traders were seen among the crowds, buying gifts for their families on the other side of the world. It seemed then as if life would go on forever.

"You never told me half this stuff!" teased Bai Dong. He was born fifteen years after his father had established his business and married a shy young woman from the same street.

"Unlike my sisters, I wasn't a clever child, was I, father?" Bai Dong began. "You wanted me to inherit the family business, didn't you?"

"A father can dream, can't he?" said Bai Jian. The others laughed.

Bai Dong continued. He explained that his interest in metalwork started when he was a child. At the age of fourteen, he had started work as an apprentice in the bronze works east of the Chinese market, almost on the quayside where his sisters and mother had been taken days before. There, he learned to cast simple tin Buddha figures, sold in their hundreds to pilgrims making their way to Ayutthaya's great temples. At twenty, he was allowed to move on to larger, seated Buddha castings in bronze and, when the threat of Burmese invasion grew ever higher, he crossed the river to the Imperial cannon foundry, where he produced firearms in bronze and iron. With his huge hands he cast small, exquisitely detailed cannon that could be fixed to the bow of a ship or even the saddle of a war elephant. Many found their way into the Royal Armouries and were later confiscated by the Burmese army.

"I grew up under the constant promise of war with the Burmese," Bai Dong explained. "Stories of their atrocities became talk of the street. I remember saying to my fellow workers that one day I would take revenge. Well, I've started."

Bai Dong turned to Mohamad and slapped him on the shoulder. "So, what about you then, what's *your* story? Tell us what's in that bag of yours – you seem to take it everywhere. Is it magic or something?"

"Oh, there's no magic in there. My story is very different to yours, though. I'm not Chinese, for a start."

"Really?" joked Bai Dong.

"My family came from Persia. My great-grandfather travelled with an embassy sent by the first King Suleiman to the Court of Narai the Great at Ayutthaya, almost exactly one hundred years ago. He had worked in the royal kitchens in our capital city of Isfahan for many years and eagerly accepted the post of embassy chef. My own father remembered being told about a fearsome journey across the ocean from Persia to a place called Mergui. It sounds as if almost everyone on the ship nearly died at some point!"

"Where's Mergui?" asked Bai Dong.

"It's an old port on the west coast. Foreign traders used to sail fully laden from India, across the Bay of Bengal to Mergui, then offload their cargo onto smaller river boats and sail up the local river until they reached the foot of the Tenasserim mountains. Then they had to transfer everything to elephants and trek over the mountains to Petchaburi on the east coast, reload *again* onto ships, cross the Gulf of Siam to the mouth of the Chao Phraya and then sail up to Ayutthaya. Can you believe it?

"My father told me it was the quickest way to get to Ayutthaya from Europe. Sailing around the Malay Peninsula, across the South China Sea and up the Gulf of Siam took many months in those days with unreliable winds and seas. But it was a terrible journey across the mountains, by all accounts – elephants sliding in mud, cargo tumbling down mountains, people dying from horrible diseases, tiger attacks, all sorts of terrible fates. My great-grandfather must have wondered why on earth he ever agreed to go.

"After many months of travel, the Embassy finally reached the Royal Court and was well received by the Emperor. People still kept dying of diseases they'd picked up on the journey, but I think some trade deals were sealed and eventually the Persians went home the same way they came. But not my great-grandfather; he and a couple of others were allowed to stay. Emperor Narai quite liked Persian food, so he hired him to work in the royal kitchens. He had brought with him a collection of recipes from Persia and kept careful notes as he adapted them to suit the Imperial Court's tastes."

He carefully lifted one of the manuscripts from its bag. "And this is the result." He thumbed through the parchment sheets. "The other book is part of our holy scripture. Much of it was apparently lost down the side of a mountain during the journey across from Mergui. It is a most rare and exquisite fragment."

The other men gazed in disbelief.

"My grandfather was born in Ayutthaya five years after the Embassy left. He grew up working in the kitchens. So did my father, and then it was my turn. And my oldest son was destined to be a cook too. Each time we invented a new dish or changed an old family recipe, we updated our book. We did that a lot – we just couldn't get hold of Persian ingredients and had to use whatever we could lay our hands on in the markets.

"We hid it so no one could ever find it. Would you believe it, we managed to convince the monks at the Royal Garden Monastery to allow us to keep it in their own reading room, facing our Holy City of Mecca?"

Jiang Xin raised an eyebrow. "In a Buddhist monastery? How did you get away with that?!"

"We needed somewhere that no one could possibly find. So, we hid our Persian books in a Buddhist monastery! The other day, after I had sent my family to the quayside thinking they would escape, I ran straight there, grabbed the family treasure… and, well, here I am and here are my beloved books. But gone is my precious family."

Jiang Xin stroked his chin. "Then as I see it, you have only one task, my friend," he suggested. "You must return your books. Not to Ayutthaya. To Persia. It is the right thing for you to do."

25

CARBON DATING

From: Sarah Richardson >s.y.richardson@london.ac.uk
To: Gordon Macallister >gordon.macallister1@ox.ac.uk
Cc:
Date: 26.03.20 11.45
Att:
Subject: A challenge

Dear Dr Macallister

I hope you don't mind me contacting you. I got your name from a recent paper on the use of radiocarbon dating in ancient parchment manuscripts. I am currently doing a PhD in London and as part of my research have identified a potentially important document written in ink on parchment. Stylistically it appears to be from the 17th–18th centuries. If I can confirm its age, its contents are going to be really important. Can I ask if you might help me get a date for this manuscript?

Thanks for reading this and I hope to hear from you soon.

Kind regards
Sara Richardson
PhD Student
University of London

From: Gordon Macallister >gordon.macallister1@ox.ac.uk
To: Sara Richardson >s.y.richardson@london.ac.uk
Cc:
Date: 28.03.18 23.20
Att:
Subject: Re: A challenge

Dear Sara

Good to hear from you. What an interesting question.

Yes, it is possible to have a look at your original manuscript to see if we can get you a date for the parchment. We have some experience doing this. In fact, the technology we have developed is quite reliable and surprisingly accurate since the collagens in the parchment tend to be extremely contemporaneous with the manuscript's text. Put simply, the goat was killed not long before its skin was written on...

It's a bit fiddly, since the surfaces of the parchment are usually filthy with time and crud, but we have worked up a treatment that removes that without disrupting the parchment's structure.

If we prove that your parchment is 17th–18th century, it doesn't prove that it was actually written on at that time. There are some hoaxes in the literature where old parchment or canvas has been written or painted on more recently. But I have a trick up my sleeve for you. I have been doing some work on dating written text. Old ink has a lot of carbon in it (it was made from things like boiled acorns) and I have a highly sensitive extraction method that only requires a tiny sample. We control for the accumulation of dirt by taking multiple samples, which are almost invisible to the naked eye.

I think the best thing to do would be for you to come up to our lab with your manuscript and I can take samples from a few places. If that sounds good, and if your institution is happy for me to do that, would you liaise with Ann, my secretary (a.c.dale@ox.ac.uk), to get a slot in my diary? I'm in Chicago at the moment but will be back in a few days.

The cost of this will be covered by one of my grants. How's that for collaboration? The deal will be co-authorship if you publish your findings, if that's OK? It would be good to be able to show that these two techniques give reproducible and reliable results in different manuscripts.

Best wishes
Gordon

Dr Gordon Macallister
Reader in Applied Isotope Chemistry
Department of Physics
Oxford University

26

THE OM NON

The old river was overhung by ancient forest branches that fractured the evening sunlight into a thousand shimmering flecks skimming across the water's surface, picking out swarms of insects dancing in the warm air. They heard voices, carried upstream from a monastery at the water's edge. A small group of monks came into view, surprised to see a boat heading towards them. They stood nervously, ready to run.

"Holy brothers, we are peaceful men who mean you no harm!" shouted Jiang Xin from the prow. Then, as the sampan neared the monastery, he added, "We escaped from Ayutthaya."

The monks immediately responded with cries of joy, rushing down to the river to meet them. Conversation soon turned to where the men were heading.

"Don't go much further down the Chao Phraya," the eldest monk said. "It is still too dangerous. The Burmese have fortresses on either side of the river at Thonburi.

Nothing can pass between them. You wouldn't stand a chance of reaching the sea that way." He described a river channel five miles downstream called the Om Non. This narrow channel flowed west into the rice fields and fruit orchards of Nonthaburi before doubling back to the Chao Phraya. From the furthest western point on the Om Non, by the Bat Temple, they could pick up an old canal connecting cross country to the Tha Chin River.

"It's a few days' travel but it's perfectly safe. Follow the Tha Chin south to the sea at the port of Mahachai. The Burmese didn't stay there, although they helped themselves to the townsfolk. You will be able to find shelter and food there, maybe even find a ship to take you wherever you wish."

The Om Non's entrance was, just as the monk had described, at the end of a straight section of river. It ran through dense thickets of nipa palms, whose tall branches curved upwards and towards the centre of the river channel, creating a shaded cavern-like corridor through the forest in which the only sounds were the rhythmic splash of Bai Dong's oar in the still brown water and the occasional shrieks from monkeys watching from their hiding places in the shadows. At times, the palms thinned to reveal hidden emerald fields, orange groves and small riverside shrines. Tiny canals branched from the main channel, some clogged with lotus or fallen palms, others leading into glimpses of paradise.

It took just three hours to reach the Bat Temple. Under

the palm canopy, the hot, humid stillness made for an uncomfortable journey. The vegetation slowly thinned to reveal a jumble of riverside houses built around narrow alleyways leading down to the water's edge. Crowds of villagers busied themselves with daily routines, calling children to supper, unloading supplies from canoes, washing clothes. Just beyond the village was a large temple clearing surrounded by ornate brick walls. Inside stood an open-sided prayer hall topped with a roof of red and gold tiles; behind it, the main temple rose on carved columns, topped with richly decorated stupas that towered above the forest canopy. Inside the temple's dark interior, lit only by candles, a huge reclining Buddha gazed out at a scene untouched by violence. Mohamad watched monks kneeling in the courtyard in front of the temple, just as he had on his last day in Ayutthaya, and heard the familiar sound of Buddhist prayer.

By the time the sampan was tethered, the pink sky around the temple stupas had become filled with hundreds of bats – thousands, perhaps – their screeches combining into a rhythmic, high-pitched throb. The men stood, looking up, scarcely able to comprehend the spectacle.

Bai Jian walked across to a small wooden office building opposite the temple and spoke to the duty priest who was sitting behind a desk, smoking a small pipe of tobacco. He briefly retold the story of the past few days, explaining that a monk in the temple at Ko Kret had directed them this way to find the Bang Yai Canal.

"Well, you've found it." The priest grinned and pointed the stem of his pipe towards the main temple building. "It starts from behind the perimeter wall and runs west for many miles. You have a long journey yet, my friend." He stood, took Bai Jian's arm and guided him out of the office. "Come, you need a good place to sleep, and food in your bellies."

27

APARTMENT 1005

The door crashes open. They immediately know that someone has died in there.

The unmistakable, sweet stench of recent death catches Kongsin by surprise as he enters the apartment, pistol high and ready. A long, dark blood smear on the wall to his left leads him to the splatter of scalp, blood and shattered brain, all that remains of whoever has been shot here. He quickly sweeps the apartment. Empty. In the bedroom, an open wardrobe, clothes scattered over the bed.

Someone has left in a hurry.

28

RESULTS

From: Gordon Macallister >g.macallister1@ox.ac.uk
To: Sara Richardson >s.y.richardson@london.ac.uk
Cc:
Date: 03.05.18 10.31
Att: richardson_manuscript_techdoc1.pdf
Subject: Radioisotope results

Dear Sara

Re: Radioisotope dating results from antique parchment document

Thank you again for coming to Oxford on 10th April when I was able to sample your manuscript for radioisotope dating. As you know, I took a small number of 0.5mm punch biopsies from tight up against the stitching in the right-hand margin on pages 2, 5, 8 and 12 where the soiling was minimal. I applied a chemical treatment to clean the surface before a collagen extraction and purification step.

In addition, I used a new micro-suction biopsy technique to remove twenty spots of ink from five sites on the same pages. These were dissolved in a chemical solvent, which stabilised the ink compounds. These samples were subjected to carbon-14 dating analysis. The scientific data are enclosed in the technical document, which is a bit of a dense read, but to summarise for you, all five biopsied pages give a very reproducible date of between 1650 and 1680 for the parchment, so this material is definitely from the 17th century, as you had hoped.

The ink sampling has given a fascinating result and you will be interested to know that this is the first time we have seen anything like this. Four partially overlapping date clusters have emerged with tight statistical probability:

1680–1700 CE – this appears to correspond with the original text.

1690–1730 CE – this corresponds to a second handwriting style.

1730–1750 CE – this corresponds to a third handwriting style.

1770–1800 CE – this corresponds to a fourth handwriting style.

All of these data, taken together with Professor Morad's stylistic comments, are consistent with a document originally written by one person some time between 1680 and 1700 and subsequently added to by three other people before 1800.

Please let me know if you would like to discuss this.

Shall we write it up for publication?
Best wishes
Gordon

Dr Gordon Macallister
Reader in Applied Isotope Chemistry
Department of Physics
Oxford University

29

THE BANG YAI CANAL

The Chinese men went to the temple early and asked for Buddha's blessing for the journey ahead. Mohamad went to find a quiet place outside the temple wall to kneel and pray alone, away from the others. He hoped one day to rekindle his faith; it had certainly been tested to breaking point. He asked himself what God would allow such destruction of life. Maybe faith would provide an answer but today Mohamad felt nothing as he knelt in the dust, thinking of his family.

As they left the Bat Temple, light from the rising sun turned the Bang Yai canal into a narrow golden thread of water that disappeared before the horizon into a misty landscape of rich green fields and plantations. From time to time they stopped at canal-side villages and spoke to families working in the fields. Few could comprehend the story they heard. Their rural life had hardly been touched by war.

There was a healing stillness in the flat, empty landscape. It took only three days to reach the Tha Chin

River under clear skies, with no need to hide from view during the day. They stopped for the night at the end of the canal. Bai Jian lit a fire, made fresh tea and grilled freshwater fish from the canal. As the night closed around them, they once again shared stories and laughed until their bellies were sore.

"So, tell me, Mohamad Mirkazemi, what was it like working in the Imperial kitchens?"

"Hot! We used to cook in these huge bronze pans set over open fires. We had everything at our disposal – every spice you could ever wish for, fresh meat, fish, the sweetest onions you can imagine, fruit – and of course, the best rice."

Bai Jian pointed out that the Emperor controlled the rice markets and always kept the best for himself.

"Wouldn't *you* if you were Emperor? Imagine being able to do whatever you want!"

"So, what was his favourite meal?" Bai Jian continued.

"There's a family story about my great-grandfather cooking a meal for the Persian Embassy visit. One day, Emperor Narai just turned up at the kitchen unannounced, took a spoon and sampled my grandfather's food. He was instantly addicted. He loved the recipes from Persia and those became incorporated into the Imperial Household's menus. Nara's descendants all liked rich sauces with a lot of spicy heat. So, my great-grandfather, grandfather, father and I spent our time cooking a variety of traditional Siamese dishes and some of our Persian-inspired dishes as well. Emperor Ekkathat's favourite dish was a sweet and sour meat curry made with the best of spices, coconut and bitter orange juice. It makes me drool to even think of it. It used to take a whole day to make it. The kitchen was filled with the aromas of toasted sweet spices and coconut. He used to call it his 'Muslim curry'!"

"Sounds typical of the Emperor," Jiang Xin said. "Well, I enjoyed the grilled fish tonight, that's more my style. I don't think my lowly stomach could take all that rich food."

"My friend, I would like to cook the Emperor's Muslim curry for you one day and you will be converted, I assure you! I don't think we could find all the ingredients in these fields, though. For the moment we'll have to make do with these simple meals."

30

PROFESSOR BAMRUNG

From: *Sara Richardson >s.y.richardson@london.ac.uk*
To: *Jatupol Bamrung >JB03@rama9.ac.th*
Cc: *Bob Oakhurst; Jenny Pulman*
Date: *05.05.18 10.20*
Att:
Subject: Ayutthaya document

Dear Professor Bamrung

I am sure you will recall your email exchange with Jenny Pulman earlier this year in which you commented that, if we were able to prove the date of our manuscript, its contents would be of great significance.

I managed to collaborate with a scientist called Gordon Macallister at Oxford University to date both the parchment and the ink and can confirm that they are both from the 17th–18th century CE. In fact, the document was started in the late 17th century CE and completed by three other people (almost certainly the original author's son, grandson and great-grandson) at different points during the 18th century CE.

I have been speaking to my PhD supervisor, Bob Oakhurst, and he has suggested I bring the document over to show you and your team to understand its importance and discuss how the news of its discovery should be handled. Does that sound reasonable? I'm happy to give a lecture/ interview/whatever.

I look forward to hearing from you.

Regards

Sara

Sara Richardson

PhD Student

University of London

31

TO MAHACHAI

The Tha Chin was a broad, quiet river fringed with floating mats of water hyacinth and groves of tall coconut palms. Although the port of Mahachai lay only twenty miles to the south, the river twisted into a seemingly endless series of switchback loops as it moved across a wide plain of rice fields, increasing the river journey to fifty miles. It took several days to reach Mahachai; long, languid days filled with nothing but the simple rhythms of life and the men's own thoughts. They would rise at dawn, throw out nets to catch fish or river shrimp, float on the current for many hours, talk now and then, tie up for the night, eat and sleep under the starry heavens.

Mahachai was built on a peninsula created by the last bend in the river. The men approached from the north late one evening. The still river air was suddenly freshened by a salty breeze from the coast. The noise of countless busy lives and the smells from a thousand kitchens floated out across the water from stilted homes and private jetties. As they rounded the tip of the peninsula, the river widened into a broad, marshy estuary lined with wooden quays and jostling ships, fishing boats, huge warehouses and temple spires, outlined against the darkening indigo sky.

Chi She managed to manoeuvre the sampan between square-rigged trading junks to a mooring post underneath a crowded fish market built on stilts over the river. Above them, baskets of every kind of fish and shrimp were being arranged on reed mats in front of cross-legged merchants, argued over in great detail by hordes of townsfolk who had descended to buy their evening meals. Around the market, street hawkers wrapped in clouds of aromatic steam sold noodles and seafood grilled over charcoal fires. Low light from paper lanterns picked out the local faces, mostly Chinese, young and old, smooth and wrinkled.

"This is chaos!" yelled Chi She above the din.

Jiang Xin smiled. "I know, isn't it fantastic? It's just like home! Let's see what we can find here." With a bound, Jiang Xin left the sampan and strode into the crowds with great purpose. The others followed, Mohamad carrying his manuscripts in their goatskin bag rather than leaving them in the sampan. They bought fresh beer and hot thick noodles in green onion broth seasoned with thick, dark soy sauce, and for a precious moment they were free of their nightmares, transported back to the alleyways of Ayutthaya's Chinese Market. They slept well that night and woke early to the raucous noise of fishing boats arriving with overnight catches from the Gulf of Siam, surrounded by swooping clouds of shrieking gulls.

Over breakfast, Mohamad suggested they ought to find a shipping office to find a trading ship prepared to take them as passengers away from Siam. This idea provoked an unexpected debate.

"What's the hurry?" asked Jiang Xin. "This is a fine place to stay. No one would ever ask us where we are from. We blend in; we belong here."

"I can't stay," Mohamad replied. "As you said, it is my duty to return these books to Persia. Stay if you like, but I will have to go."

The sampan fell silent. Mohamad gazed out over the salt flats, imagining what lay over the horizon.

Bai Jian spoke first. "Personally, I agree with Jiang Xin. For me this is a perfect place to spend the rest of my life. I may not find work as a lacquer painter here but there will be paid work and I can build a new life. I think Bai Dong would feel the same."

Bai Dong nodded, his gaze turned away from Mohamad, who spoke next.

"I understand. This town is far more like your old home than the one I seek. I think it was always possible that we would go our separate ways at some point. You must do what is right for you. Chi She, what about you?"

"I don't know. As you know, I didn't have family and have always lived on my own. I quite like the idea of escaping on a ship to some exotic far-away place. I need some time to decide."

Mohamad took his bag and stepped ashore. South of the market he could see a row of square-riggers moored against a quay, behind which was a row of busy shop houses. Each specialised in different goods: salt, rice, tea, calamac and other rare, perfumed woods.

Mohamad walked across the quay and ducked as he

entered a tea merchant's shop. The air was heavy with the sweet grassy smell of tea, arranged in zinc-plated tins and paper packets on slatted wooden shelves. Towards the rear of the shop sat a middle-aged Siamese man. He stood and walked towards Mohamad.

"Good morning, sir, how may I help you today? I have a fine aged oolong, fresh in this week from Canton. Would you like to try?"

"That's very kind, sir, but I'm not really looking for tea. I'm looking for a ship to take me to Persia."

"*Persia?* Whatever for? Come, sit with me awhile. I bet *you* have an interesting story."

The two men sat together at the back of the shop. The merchant poured boiled water from a blackened kettle onto khaki balls of tea in white porcelain cups to create a fragrant, malty infusion. Mohamad told his story while they sipped. He explained how he felt it was his duty to return his family's treasured books to Persia and how his Chinese companions had decided to stay in Mahachai.

"Well, most of the vessels at this quay come down from Hoi An with precious woods, gold or silk, and return to Saigon heavy with rice and salt," the merchant explained. "They don't usually sail west. What you need is a Dutch ship going to somewhere like Malacca or Batavia."

The merchant pulled back a curtain at the rear of the shop and shouted across a tiny courtyard. "Boon-Nam, could you run and find Mustafa from the Golden Dragon Quay?"

A young boy ran past them out into the street and reappeared minutes later with a tall, dark-skinned gentleman wearing a broad, remarkably clean, white turban.

"Ah, Mustafa! *As-salamu alaykum*, my friend. This man needs your help."

"*Wa 'alaykum*," replied the man called Mustafa. "How may I help?"

Mohamad introduced himself. "*As-salamu alaykum.* Sir, my name is Mohamad Mirkazemi. My family came here from Persia four generations ago."

"To Mahachai? Whatever had *they* done wrong?!"

"No, to Ayutthaya. We were chefs in the Imperial kitchens. I escaped from there when the Burmese attacked last month."

"Ah, I heard about that. I am sorry. Allah will be looking after you."

"It doesn't feel like it at times," Mohamad replied. "I am seeking a boat to Malacca or Batavia to help me get to Persia. Can you help me?"

"That's a *long* way, my friend. Are you sure? My European friends tell me it's an awful journey. But I can help you get to Batavia if you wish. There's a Dutch trader arriving in port any day now from Malacca with spices and cloth. The Commander might let you return with him to Batavia. It'll take a couple of days to unload and reload but you might be out of here in a week or two while the winds are still strong. Have you money to pay him?"

"Alas, my friend, I have no more money than the few old coins in my purse. I left Ayutthaya with very little. We have been looked after by kind monks and farmers for weeks, eating whenever we can."

Mustafa looked across at the tea merchant and winked. "Come to the Golden Dragon Quay in two days' time and I'll introduce you to Commander Vos. We'll see if we can negotiate free board. Don't say a word until I have spoken to him; he can be a tricky character, like most Europeans in these parts. Depends how much gin he's had."

Mohamad thanked Mustafa and the tea merchant and walked back out into the street.

The tea merchant turned to Mustafa and laughed. "*Vos*? Really? I'd hate to spend any time at sea with that one!"

"I suppose desperate times call for desperate measures..." Mustafa grinned. "Anyhow, Vos owes me a favour."

32

AN INVITATION

From: Jatupol Bamrung >JB03@rama9.ac.th
To: Sara Richardson >s.y.richardson@london.ac.uk
Cc: Bob Oakhurst; Jenny Pulman
Date: 05.05.18 10.20
Att:
Subject: Re: Ayutthaya document

Dear Sara

This is amazing news! Actually, it's the discovery of the century, as far as I am concerned. It moves our cultural history on a leap and will be of enormous interest to many people in this country.

Yes, do come over. It's very hot here at the moment but send me some possible dates and I'll help you sort out some accommodation. See if Bob Oakhurst can get your travel costs reimbursed. I'll get you to present your findings at one of our department's evening lectures (you get a free meal after that!) and of course you will just have to go up to Ayutthaya. I think we should do some media work while you are here too (don't be too alarmed!).

I am a great believer that nothing happens in this world without a reason. You were meant to find this document. It was already decided. It's now your task to bring it home. It's had an amazing journey so far, don't you think? I'd love to know how it ended up in Malacca – I guess we may never know.

Anyway, I look forward to hearing from you.
Best wishes
JB

Prof Dr Jatupol Bamrung
Professor of History
King Rama IX University
Bangkok
Thailand

33

THE FOX AND THE OLD ORANGE TREE

Jan van Mensburg – known as 'Vos' to most people after his long, copper-coloured, non-regulation ponytail, which many compared to the tail of a fox – stood alone on the top deck of his beloved three-masted square-rigger, the *Oud Oranjeboom*, staring down through his pocket telescope at the quayside. Over his camisole shirt he wore a red, tailed broadcloth frock coat, lavishly embroidered with golden thread. With his clean white stockings and knee breeches fastened at the knees with gold buckles, his six-foot-tall European frame towered, glittering, above most other men.

Vos, now almost fifty, was a well-seasoned Commander of Dutch East India Company trading vessels. His quiet manner and hawkish eye could be deceptive; most people on the seas knew about his reputation for terrible outbursts of intolerance and violent punishment, often fuelled by rough Batavian gin. Those who worked on his ships treated him with respect and suspicion in equal measure, and with rare exception remained loyal to him for many years in order to avoid his wrath. Born in 1730 in his father's step-gabled, red-brick house in the port town of Enthuizen on the Zuyderzee, he joined the VOC as third mate at the age of seventeen, just like the five generations of men before him, rising through the ranks to Captain by his mid-twenties and Commander a few years later.

Vos considered the *Oud Oranjeboom* to be his own home. He captained her maiden voyage from Texel to Batavia in 1752, an arduous sea journey of two hundred and forty days in which eleven men died before even reaching Cape Town. She had seen four further round trips between Texel and Batavia via Bengal, three of them commanded by Vos, but was now in semi-retirement, plying the seas and waterways between Batavia and Ayutthaya via the Straights ports of Malacca and Johor. Vos had commanded other return voyages between Holland and Batavia in the VOC vessels *Haarlem* and *Damzicht* – grueling, dangerous journeys in which many men had died and Vos himself had twice narrowly missed death from fever before deciding that his long-voyage days were over. With typical skill, he had managed to convince the VOC Chamber back in Amsterdam that they needed a senior Commander to permanently oversee the domestic Eastern trading routes. They had agreed, and Vos had been given responsibility for his old favourite, the *Oud Oranjeboom*, in her retirement. Vos lived on the sea, preferring to spend as little time as possible ashore, and he knew every trader in every port. They made it their business to know him, too.

Mustafa Farooq, resplendent in blue robe and white turban, stood on the quayside and waved at his old friend Vos, who had already spotted him in his telescope.

"My good friend, Commander van Mensburg, how do I find you today?" he bellowed.

"Most excellent, Mr Farooq, thank you, most excellent – and in need of a little tea and fresh bread this fine morning!" Vos shouted over the taffrail, walking briskly to the gangplank. Having secured a feathered, tricornered hat to his head, he strode down to the quayside and embraced Farooq as an old friend.

"Took a bashing out there this time. Very stormy off the Malay coast at one point. But all is good and no one died for a change! Your men will find everything in order, mainly Indian cloth this time, I think. And cinnamon. It smells wonderful in there." He passed a rolled inventory to Farooq, who briefly inspected it, rerolled it and passed it to his aide, two steps to his rear.

Farooq rubbed his hands together. "Let's have this unloaded quickly then!" he shouted at the aide. "Now then, Commander, let me get you some tea."

Inside Farooq's warehouse was a large and airy office furnished in the European style and hung with richly coloured Bengali fabrics. Frankincense burned in a brass dish in the middle of the room, filling the air with its intoxicating scent. Vos removed his hat and shoes at the door and collapsed into an armchair, stretching out his legs.

Farooq began his hospitality. "My good friend, the tea merchant, has sourced a very fine oolong tea this week, if that's to your liking? Good, and I'll get you some bread. I presume you will dine with my family tonight?"

"Of course. A highlight of my travels. Invitation very gratefully received," Vos replied, and yawned.

Farooq barked an order through the heavy curtain at the rear of his office, and moments later his wife appeared with a tray of hot tea, flatbreads, oil and dates, which she placed before Vos on a low teak table. For the next hour, the two men spoke of business matters, sipping their tea, debating the current price of commodities and discussing new trading opportunities. Farooq explained the terrible news from Ayutthaya and reassured Vos that his regular supplies of nutmegs and silk would be unaffected – although, he joked, the supply of elephants was likely to be a problem for some time. A new supply of pepper was opening up from northern Siam, he explained, a very different product from the corns imported from India. He passed Vos a sample of the fragrant pepper, stitched into a cloth packet.

"Try them with some good fatty meat," he advised. "But not ship's biscuits."

Financial matters then followed, both men respectfully challenging each other's prices while making a perfectly reasonable profit from each other.

Vos stood and stretched. "I should supervise the offloading, my friend. Thank you for your hospitality, Mustafa, the tea was most excellent. I will see you later."

"Of course." Farooq smiled broadly. "I'll send someone to collect you from your ship and bring you to my house at sundown." He escorted Vos out of the warehouse and onto the quay. Vos's imposing presence stiffened sinews around him; the ship's crew and local warehousemen alike stood to attention as he walked past them back to the gangplank.

"Carry on, men. No slacking," he jabbed. "There's a job to be done here. When you have finished, you may do as you wish, as long as I don't find out about it." He pointed to the third mate who stood, stripped to the waist, barrow in hand. "Get a bloody wash, will you, de Vries? And *behave* yourself tonight, for God's sake. If I have to send the First Mate to find you in some stinking brothel again, I'll personally tie you to the main mast and thrash the flesh from your bones!" De Vries knew this was only meant in half jest; everyone on board feared the whip. Vos, when drunk and seething with uncontrollable rage in the middle of the ocean, had used the whip before. Few recipients had survived the assault without loss of limb or eye.

At sundown, after a brief but heavy storm that still echoed to the east, Vos was met on the quayside by Farooq's aide, who greeted him formally and led him through the alleyways and busy streets behind the waterfront to Farooq's family home. Farooq was one of the richest and most popular of the international traders in Mahachai and had amassed a considerable fortune from selling the finest silks and spices to the Portuguese and Dutch. His house, a two-storey European fashion statement matched by few others in the town, lay on a quiet street, set behind a small courtyard planted with lipstick palms and potted *strelitzia*, a new and exotic import from the Western Cape. He had spared no expense in securing the latest architectural features: Dutch-styled gables, an arched palisade on the front elevation supporting a broad veranda on the upper floor, a clay tiled roof and louvred shutters painted in the most fashionable green. Vos was deeply impressed.

"This is a fine house indeed, my friend. You have impeccable taste," he commented, passing him a gift of boxed tobacco. Farooq accepted the gift gracefully and proudly introduced Vos to his family, who stood in line to receive their honoured guest.

"Come," he said. "Let us sit while our meal is prepared."

The two men sat on Indian cushions sipping sweet rose-infused tea, exchanging tales. Vos entertained Farooq with descriptions of Batavia, Bengal and Cape Town. Farooq responded with detailed descriptions of the Burmese attack on Ayutthaya.

"It's a tragedy," Vos noted. "It was quite unlike any other city I have ever visited. How anyone survived is quite beyond me."

Farooq saw his opportunity. "Well, in fact I met a man last week who *had* managed to escape. The Emperor's chef, no less. He told vivid tales of how the city met its end. He and a number of other men managed to capture a boat, bring it down the Chao Phraya, cross open countryside to the Tha Chin and down to Mahachai."

Vos raised an eyebrow, impressed. "A brave and difficult journey indeed. These must be very determined men."

"I will introduce him to you tomorrow, if I may. He

is called Mr Mohamad Mirkazemi. He is hoping to find a ship willing to take him to Batavia. Actually, he wants to return to his ancestral home in Persia."

Vos winked. "If he's a decent fellow I'm sure I can find room for him, at the right price of course."

Farooq leaned forward and looked Vos in the eye. "Which is where I would like to call in a favour, Commander, if I might. You will remember that I managed to secure a particularly good personal deal for you last year? Do you remember? Those bails of wonderful yellow silk that had come down from Hoi An? If I recall correctly, I also threw in two large boxes of ray skins, two barrels of salt and a sack of premium-quality jasmine rice for good measure. Was that not so?"

"Ah, yes. Generous gifts indeed, Mr Farooq." Vos knew that there was really no such thing as a free gift. "And in return, of course I would be happy to take your Mr Mirkazemi to Batavia. As long as he is a decent man and is not going to make trouble on my ship."

Farooq extended a slender arm and shook Vos firmly by the hand. "You have my word, sir, and you can make your own assessment of Mr Mirkazemi in the morning. You are a very fine gentleman. It is always an honour to do business with you. Now – dinner!"

34

A MEETING

Morning was often a spectacular event in Mahachai. Vos stood on the quarter deck, looking south over the port rail towards the river estuary, a slender clay tobacco pipe pinched between thumb and forefinger, inhaling its mellow fragrant smoke. By now, a warm land breeze had started to blow from the north. The rippled river surface reflected a dance of silver sunlight on the hulls of ships moored alongside the *Oud Oranjeboom*. Shrill cries from marshland birds, racing low across the river, pierced the flat silence. *Not so different from home*, Vos thought to himself as he turned to look across the main deck, down towards the quayside. There were his men, already at work unloading the remaining cargo from the hold. There too was de Vries, fully clothed this time and looking well-rested. Vos stepped nimbly down the steps to the main deck and strode over to him.

"De Vries, what a pleasant surprise! What did you get up to last night?"

"Sir, I was a model citizen and a credit to your good name, of course. A small group of us went to explore the market and found some good entertainment there."

"I can quite imagine, de Vries. Spare me the fine detail, if you will. I'm just glad you're all here in one piece. Now, we're taking on a lot of cargo this time – make sure the boys do a good job, will you? Keep it well balanced. Mr Farooq's men should have everything out of the warehouse onto the quay by noon. With luck we'll be away the day after tomorrow at the latest." Vos tapped out his pipe on the ship's rail, fixed his hat to his head, buttoned his frock coat and walked down the gangplank to the quay. Farooq's aide greeted him again with an excessively ornate bow and escorted him to the warehouse office, where Farooq was already drinking tea with a slightly built, rather nervous-looking man. They both stood as Vos entered the room.

"Ah, Mr Farooq," said Vos, removing his hat with a swoop. "May I thank you again for a very fine meal and excellent hospitality last evening. You have a magnificent home and a most magnificent wife, if I may say. Both the envy, surely, of your neighbours!"

"It was our pleasure, sir," Farooq replied. "You are always most welcome." He paused briefly. "May I now introduce you to Mr Mohamad Mirkazemi, an Imperial chef and a citizen of Ayutthaya? We spoke about him last night." Mohamad extended his hand in greeting and Vos shook it firmly.

"Mr Farooq here tells me that you managed to escape the attack on Ayutthaya. It's a city I have grown to know and love. Such a tragedy. Tell me, sir, why do you wish to return to Persia? It is a long and arduous journey, not for the faint of heart."

"Commander," Mohamad began, "as you may know, the city I called my home has been destroyed, reduced to nothing but charred timber and brick ruins. I have seen terrible things, sir. I can never return."

"And you wish me to take you to Batavia, sir?"

"If you are able, I would be indebted to you forever."

"There will be no debt, sir, please consider this my pleasure and duty. Come with me, sir, let me introduce you to the First Mate, Mr Willem de Jonge. He will find you a place to call home until we reach Batavia. In return, maybe you can cook us some of your royal food, eh? I seek nothing more from you. To be honest, the ship's food is generally awful. We could do with a change."

Farooq beamed at his friend and opened his arms wide. "This is a most magnificent gesture! Sirs, I will personally see to it that you have all the food supplies you need for your journey. Mr Mirkazemi, perhaps you would be kind enough to speak to my aide and provide him with a list of everything you require?" He turned and shouted at the curtain at the rear of his office. "More tea!"

Willem de Jonge had worked his way up from Third to First Mate under Vos's often challenging command over the past six year, always – apart from a voyage home to Amsterdam in late 1765 – on the *Oud Oranjeboom*. He had developed a soft spot for her aged, creaking timbers, knew every inch of her one hundred and twenty feet, and had worked out exactly how to guide her through the seas and river channels around the Siamese Gulf and Malay Peninsula. Thirty long-serving, highly experienced and loyal VOC employees made up the permanent crew; most were Dutch, with additional crew members taken on as needed from time to time, usually from local port towns along the way.

As he stepped on board the *Oud Oranjeboom*, Mohamad immediately noticed the appalling smell: damp and sour from waterlogged timber, mould, sodden rope, human sweat and sewage.

De Jonge noticed him wince and laughed. "I see you have noticed the ripe stink of a working ship, Mr Mohamad. You'll get used to it in no time at all. She's due a good clean down when we get back to Batavia. Let me explain where everything is." He stamped his foot. "We're standing on the main deck. Below us is the orlop, or lower deck. That's where the crew sleeps when not on duty. The galley is down there, too.

"Behind us is the main cabin accommodation for senior crew members and the steering room. You see the steps leading up beside the door? They lead to the quarter deck and the upper cabin where Vos has his office and personal quarters. Then above that is the poop deck and a small topmost cabin, which we don't generally use. On long voyages we have been known to keep chickens up there, though."

Mohamad raised his eyebrows. "Chickens?"

De Jonge sensed the next question. "I know what you are going to ask – you'll have to ask the boss. He's never been keen on the idea of chickens shitting on his roof." He took Mohamad by the arm. "Come, let me show you to your quarters."

Ducking through a low door, the two men entered the main cabin area. Vos and other VOC commanders alike allowed guests on board at their own discretion (and in Vos's case, he usually refused). Mohamad was allocated a simple room in the front of the main cabin area with a bed, window, washstand and mirror.

"You're next to me, so no snoring. Vos thinks you are some sort of royalty, so we've even sorted out a chamber pot for you."

"Where does everyone else... you know? *Excrete?*" asked Mohamad, timidly.

De Jonge laughed. "The rest of us have to use the 'seats of convenience' in the heads." He pointed to a row of toilet seats suspended over each side of the ship's bow. "Ordinary crew dangle to starboard and officers to port. It's fine in quiet waters, hanging over the side, but the moment the sea whips up your bare arse – I'll leave that to your imagination, but suffice it to say we don't have enough buckets on board for men to use in moments like that. The Commander, of course, has his own toilet up top."

"Of course. Mr de Jonge, thank you for providing me with such luxurious accommodation. It's more than I could have wished for."

"You are clearly a man of simple pleasures. Let's go down to the orlop and find de Groot, the cook. Most of the smell on board seems to come from him these days. I'm sure he's started to rot from the inside."

De Jonge led Mohamad down a narrow ladder to the still, lamp-lit orlop. The hot, damp air reeked. A pale, gaunt man with blackened teeth and oily hair was sitting in the gloom, peeling onions by candlelight. He looked up with disdain, clearly unimpressed at being disturbed. De Jonge explained that Mr Mirkazemi was a chef from the Imperial Siamese Court and was joining the *Oud Oranjeboom* for the return voyage to Batavia, during which Commander van Mensburg expected him to share cooking duties.

"What does he know about cooking on a bloody ship?" the cook spat, flinging his knife to the floor.

"I would kindly remind you, Mr de Groot," said De Jonge, "that this gentleman is a guest of the Commander and is here to help you. You would do well to rein in your lob-tongue, sir. Mr Mirkazemi will be cooking in the *Siamese* style. We will have a welcome break from your endless salt pork and peas. Watch and learn, sir. Watch and learn." He turned to Mohamad. "Mr Mirkazemi, Mr de Groot has been our loyal ship's cook for five years and, apart from a tendency to descend to the lowest tolerable levels of language, he is in fact very experienced and will help you adapt your recipes to cooking in these squalid conditions. Won't you, Mr de Groot?"

"Aye, if it pleases you, sir," de Groot sneered, touching his forelock in mock respect for the First Mate. "Come on then, Mr Mockazoomo—"

"Mirkazemi."

"Like I say. I'll take you on a tour."

Mohamad stood at the entrance to the galley – a small room, no more than six feet in length and just four feet wide, completely lined with copper plate. In the middle of the ceiling was a wide chimney, which also served as a limited source of daylight. Firebricks lined the floor and the walls up to waist height; a large scorch in the floor marked the hearth of an open cooking fire, around which were arranged a number of wrought iron pot stands.

"You manage to cook in here for a whole ship?" asked Mohamad, amazed.

"Aye, that we do, sir."

"Doesn't the fire burn through the floor?"

"Aye, that it sometimes does, sir. This old lady had a refit some years ago – all the floor timbers in here had to be replaced. Some were quite badly charred, I'm told. A ship from the same yard had its galley burn right down through the floor only five days out of Cape Town. The whole lot – ship, cargo, men and all – went up in flames and down to the seabed in a cloud of steam. This galley should see us out nicely, though – we've got a thick layer of salt between the copper and the brick. Belt, braces and buckles, you might say."

It was clear that life on board a VOC East Indiaman was going to be more challenging than Mohamad had imagined.

"And where do you keep supplies?"

"Down there on the port side mainly. That's where I keep my salt pork, beef, herring, sometimes tripe if the victualler can lay his hands on any. Dried peas, oatmeal and flour are down there too. Mustard, vinegar, pepper, pickled cucumbers, spices can all be found in kegs a bit further down. Vegetables I like to keep close by – they generally only last a week or two before they turn black.

Bread, biscuits, raisins and sugar I keep down in the bread room where it's dry and I can keep the door locked. Fresh water's in thirty-gallon casks stored aft here on the orlop. We have to take that on whenever we can; it doesn't stay fresh long. There are a bigger reserve casks in the hold but that often turns sour. Oh, and there's beer down here on the starboard side, two thousand gallons of it. Wine for the officers is stored up top. You'll get the hang of it once we set sail."

"Do you have fish?" Mohamad asked.

"Catch it as we go along, sir. Sometimes we get a sea turtle for a change."

"It's very different to what I am used to!" Mohamad laughed. "It's quite daunting, actually. I'll need somewhere to store my supplies, Mr Boot."

"De Groot."

"Like I said, sir."

De Groot smiled. Both men, with no common experience other than the heat of a cooking fire, knew they would get on just fine.

Mohamad considered the journey ahead, the men on board the ship and the cramped cooking facilities. He dictated a list of equipment and food supplies to the clerk from Farooq's warehouse.

"I'll need a large pestle and mortar – a stone one if possible, I have seen them in the market near here – then two large iron woks, four large steamer baskets, two long-handled cooking spatulas, one coconut scraper."

The clerk paused. "OK. That should suffice, sir. Remember the crew work in two-hour shifts, so you'll only need to feed half the crew at a time. Any more equipment like that and you'll be taking on water!"

"Excellent. Now, coconuts. Lots of them. I'd say ten picul. And rice, five picul. The best quality, please."

"That's also a lot of extra weight, sir. I'll need to check with the Commander to make sure he's happy with that."

"If you must, but there are many mouths to feed before we reach Batavia. Now, the spices. First – are you noting this down? – I'll need one picul each of garlic, shallots and salt. Then, ten catties each of dried long chillies, white and black peppercorns, coriander seed, green cardamom and cumin seeds; then five catties each of nutmeg, mace, dried lemongrass, dried lime leaves. Soy sauce, fish sauce. Oh, and pumpkins and green oranges – let's say one picul of each for now, if you can find them."

"Mr Mirkazemi, that's a *lot* of provisions, if I might say so," said the clerk. "This is a working ship, not a royal kitchen."

Mohamad frowned at him.

"It'll take a day or so to find all of this, you know."

"Then you'd better get on with it, sir. Oh, and I'll need one fresh veal carcass and two dozen live chickens."

"Sir, fresh meat will turn rancid within two days. You may have to use salted beef. That's easier for us to source. And the Commander doesn't allow livestock on this ship."

Mohamad considered the clerk's advice. "One fresh carcass please, if you will, and the rest can be salted. A new challenge for me. I've never had to use preserved meat before."

The clerk smiled. "Of course, sir, but then no one has ever tried to cook this sort of cuisine on board a Dutch East Indiaman. The crew on these ships get used to eating a mundane diet of salt pork with peas, salt beef with dumplings, and the occasional fish. Quite disgusting, if you ask me. Hard biscuit on longer journeys when everything else runs out. It's a miracle these men are still alive. Those that haven't already died of sea scurvy or rot, of course. At least this ship will visit a number of ports along the way so you can restock with fresh goods."

Mohamad shook the clerk's hand and returned to the ship. The clerk stalked off to the market, muttering to himself, to begin the process of stocking Mr Mirkazemi's lavish kitchen. He doubted whether Mr Farooq had any idea – or the slightest care – what a huge bill he would be handed once the *Oud Oranjeboom* had disappeared over the horizon.

35

A FLIGHT TO BANGKOK

Friday 11th August 2020

Sara has never travelled further than Rome on her own before. Ordinarily, although she enjoys her own company more than anyone else's, the prospect of an eleven-hour long-haul flight would be a daunting prospect, but today she fizzes with excitement as she turns and waves at her beaming parents from Heathrow's Terminal 5 security gate. With Bob Oakhurst's help, she won a travelling scholarship to present the Siamese manuscript to the history faculty at Rama IX University in Bangkok. Ahead lays adventure, opportunity and the next stage of her career.

Once through security, Sara shops briefly for magazines, mineral water and chocolate before settling down to wait for her flight. The terminal building is bursting with travellers from every corner of the world – each, she imagines, with a story and a purpose, although surely none as interesting as hers. She sits, wedged between sleeping bodies, one hand on her rucksack. Inside, wrapped carefully in bubble plastic, is the manuscript. *How strange*, she muses, *that it took over two hundred years for this fragile document to find its way to London by sea and land, only to return now in a matter of hours on a plane.*

The flight fills slowly. There are the usual small-scale international battles over hand luggage and seat allocations. Sara places her own bag in the overhead locker above her with enormous care and takes her aisle seat deep within the crowding Economy cabin. She winces as her neighbour stuffs his own hand luggage alongside hers. He smiles at her when she stands to reorganise the locker to her own liking.

"Sorry, I'm not very tidy. Major problem," he explains.

Sara blushes. "No, no, I'm sorry – it's just I have something fragile in my bag, I just wanted to make sure it's OK. You must think... Sorry." She blushes for a second time.

"I'm Connor," he says. A mild Irish accent. "I hope you don't mind me talking to you, I'm nervous about flying. Since we're going to be sat next to each other for the next eleven hours, I'll tell you my story if you tell me yours."

Sara is unused to such forwardness. Unused to small talk in general, in fact, especially with young, attractive men. She had imagined an uninterrupted journey, immersed in her thoughts. As the next few hours open up, she surprises herself at how easy it is to hold a normal conversation.

"I'm Sara. Sara Richardson." She holds out her hand awkwardly and Connor shakes it with exaggerated ceremony.

"Well, it's nice to meet you, Sara Richardson. I'm Connor McCarthy."

Sara hardly notices the plane take off as she and Connor begin the sort of fast-paced conversation that two complete strangers who meet by chance fall into, each eager to tell their story before their time together runs out. She learns of Connor's father's recent death from a brain tumour, and his plan to work his way around Asia as part of his gap year before starting a course in graphic design; he learns of Sara's quiet, intellectual upbringing and what it is like to work in the British Library. They try to watch movies but find themselves chatting aimlessly about politics, religion, literature and music as they take a crash course in each other. And then, almost as soon as their relationship has started, BA0009 lands in Bangkok and they find themselves standing, waiting to leave the plane.

"Sara, I'd love to buy you a drink while you're here," Connor blurts.

Awkward, Sara thinks to herself. She blushes. "Sure, give me your number and I'll call you when I can," she replies, knowing that she won't and that she will have forgotten about him within a day. It's one of those open-ended ways of ending such a brief and intense moment in time, as if the outpouring of their life histories, dreams and fantasies has meant nothing at all to her. He scribbles his number on his boarding pass and hands it to her.

"Thanks, Connor, I really enjoyed meeting you. I hope your trip works out for you," she says softly. They smile and leave the plane together, separating in the chaotic crowd-march through the arrivals hall towards the immigration desk. She takes a detour to a rest room, where she tears the boarding pass in two and throws it in the waste bin. Romance is absolutely out of the question. This trip is strictly academic business. She watches Connor leave the luggage hall before retrieving her own luggage, then walks through the cool terminal building to the taxi rank. Glass doors slide open and she walks into the thick morning heat. It is just after 9.30am. Sara has already agreed with Professor Bamrung that she will find her own way to her hotel and she will contact him during the day to arrange a suitable time to meet after his morning lectures.

The taxi from Suvarnabhumi takes over an hour to battle through dense, noisy expressway traffic. Bangkok reveals itself to Sara as an endless series of low-rise industrial units, roadside advertising signs, residential blocks, temples and mosques, broken every now and then by small patches of farmland, lushly planted with crops. Leaving the elevated expressway, the taxi plunges into a shaded world of shops, restaurants, small backpacker hotels, traffic fumes and, Sara notes, electric wire – miles of black wire, tied into thick bundles, wrapping around buildings, leaping over streets. Down here at street level, the city has grown old and stained with history: a golden stupa standing behind a jumble of faded, green-shuttered colonial-style buildings; a white octagonal fort, black-streaked with age and now flanked by a noisy rickshaw rank and a modern coffee house; bridges crossing ancient canals filled with still brown water. The taxi squeezes down a narrow lane opposite the Chill Out Heritage Guesthouse. At the end, before a pier jutting out into the Chao Phraya River, is Sara's hotel, inconspicuous behind a row of palm trees and a shaded garden: the Siam Palace.

Sara pays her driver and stands in the heat looking up at the faded 1970s concrete building. An avenue flanked by white lilies leads to a small shrine surrounded by drifting smoke from burning incense sticks, then on to the hotel reception, where the receptionist offers Sara iced ginger tea while she completes her check-in papers. An elderly man with bad hips takes her to a small room on the second floor with a side view over the palm trees to the river. She thanks him for his troubles and tips him generously before clicking the door shut. The antique air conditioning system breaks the silence with a low rhythmic murmur but it does at least seem to work. Sara throws herself onto the bed and laughs. Alone at last.

36

THE *OUD ORANJEBOOM* SETS SAIL

At dawn, Vos stood quietly up on the quarter deck smoking his morning pipe. He watched the spiralling tobacco smoke catch on the light north-easterly wind. Time to leave. He caught sight of the First Mate watching him from the main deck below.

"Mr de Jonge, you'll know what I am about to say."

"Indeed I do, sir." De Jonge and his Commander had worked together for long enough that they often reached the same decisions without needing to speak. A nod was often all they needed to communicate. He continued, "This breeze isn't enough to sail off the quay though, sir – we'll have to kedge out into the main channel."

"So be it. I'll be in my cabin, Willem." Vos much preferred sailing in rough open seas where most men would quake in fear. He had no interest in the tedious business of manoeuvring in and out of port and preferred to leave that to his First Mate.

Within minutes the main anchor had been raised and

the mooring lines released from the quayside. Mohamad felt the old ship drift slightly, jumped up from his bunk and ducked out onto the main deck to witness the departure. Four men rowed along the *Oud Oranjeboom's* port side in the ship's tender. In it, they carried a smaller kedging anchor attached by a long rope to a capstan up on the ship's main deck. At almost a furlong from the ship, the kedging anchor was heaved over the side of the tender onto the mud and shingle riverbed and a small flag was raised. On this signal, four crew members on board started to turn the capstan, winding in the kedging line and easing the *Oud Oranjeboom's* bow away from the quayside and out into the river channel.

While Mohamad had been watching the ship's slow departure, a crowd had started to gather behind him on the quayside. At the front, dressed immaculately in a gold robe and new jet-black turban decorated with a large, sparkling jewel, stood the imposing figure of Mr Mustafa Farooq. His clerk and warehouse team stood around him. Mohamad heard the growing noise and walked across the deck to see what was going on.

"Good luck on your voyage, Mr Mirkazemi! May Allah protect you!" he shouted. "He is watching over you. I will be praying for your safety every night!"

Mohamad started to thank him but his voice faltered as a number of familiar faces joined the crowd. The tall, slender figure of Mr Jiang, the elderly furniture maker from Ayutthaya, caught his eye first. He grinned a toothless grin at Mohamad as their gazes met, mouthed the words, "Farewell, friend," and held his palms together in prayer. Mohamad's throat thickened with sadness. Next to Mr

Jiang, Mr Chi the potter and Mr Bai Senior the lacquer painter waved their arms high in the air, cheering. Mr Bai Junior, the bronze-caster and recent double-murderer, stood at the front of the quay, his right hand held over his heart, tears streaming down his broad cheeks.

"Thank you!" he bellowed. "You saved my life. I will never forget your kindness."

Mohamad, now sobbing as the memories of past weeks rushed forward, managed to shout a farewell and thanked everyone for their help and friendship. He promised that Mirkazemis would return one day to Siam when it was safe, knowing deep within his heart that he would probably never see his country again.

By now the *Oud Oranjeboom* was drifting in the main river channel and the kedging team had been hoisted back on board. The current carried the ship slowly away from the cheering crowds. Vos stepped out of his quarters onto the main deck and waved his hat in dramatic circles.

"See you next year, Mr Farooq!" he shouted. On his instruction, men high up in the rigging let down the topgallant sails to catch the breeze, then, as the ship rounded the last bend in the river into the open estuary, the topsails were unfurled with a soft rumble, snapping taut in the wind. By now, the Golden Dragon Quay had vanished behind salt flats and haze and the ship slowly pushed out into the Siamese Gulf. Mohamad felt the ship heave forwards as the main sails were unfurled and went to find a safe spot to watch from the stern as the crew went through its familiar routine.

Throughout the morning, land thinned to a dark green line on the surface of the sea, then disappeared altogether.

Mohamad sat with his memories, breathing in the fresh air and watching waves flick and spray around the ship. For the first time in many weeks he felt a sense of deep, safe peace. Ahead, after four or five days' sailing, lay the first stop: Ligor.

37

APPLE CRUMBLE

Sara locks her camera and passport in the room safe before refreshing her face with warm water from the cold tap, then leaves the hotel and walks back up the side street to find the Sugar Cube Coffee House that she had spotted from the taxi as they passed the old fortress on the corner of the street. She sits in the fiercely air-conditioned interior and orders an iced latte and a French pastry. She calls Jatupol Bamrung, who answers cheerfully.

"Hi, Sara, you made it! How are you? Is your hotel OK? I tend to use it for all of my visitors – it's not five stars, but it's clean and comfortable, isn't it?"

"It's lovely, Professor, thank you. It'll be just fine. I can even see the river if I lean out of the window a bit. I just wanted to let you know that I am safe, and to ask what time we can meet to talk about my lecture."

"Of course. But you have plenty of time to prepare for that, you know. You should get out and explore a bit. It's not every day that you have a few days in Bangkok. I tell you what, shall we meet later today? I'm meeting with some of my students this afternoon. We often do that on a Saturday. I'll show you around the campus a bit; maybe we can grab some food? Why don't you get a taxi over to the history department and just let me know when you've arrived?"

Sara knows she'll be exhausted by the early evening but doesn't want to disappoint – and in any case, she is fascinated to meet the Professor. Jaasmin Morad had suggested that Sara read his published works on the domestic history of ancient Siam by way of background preparation for her visit. Sara had approached this with her usual rigour, carefully sourcing all of the available publications, reading them at her desk in sequence and making neat notes in a fresh pad. She soon found herself entangled in a richly imagined ancient world reconstructed using scarce documents from market traders, magistrates, monasteries and contemporaneous private diaries. During the weeks leading up to her journey east, she had left her desk, abandoned her logical methods and found herself sitting late into the evening curled on her sofa, surrounded by Bamrung's imagery, trying to imagine what he was like. He had a way of connecting with these distant historical sources as if weaving with fine silken threads bound to fleeting moments of the past, capturing them, pulling them together and preserving them. Sara had come to realise just how important her find would be to him. Professor Morad had known it but wanted Sara to work it out for herself.

Sara returns to the hotel and takes a shower, then tries to decide what a young postgrad student should wear to a first meeting with a Thai Professor whose academic output had fascinated her almost to the point of obsession. She settles on jeans, a plain white shirt and new Converse – completely the opposite of her usual attire.

Bamrung's cell phone pings. A text from Sara. *Hi, just in reception.* Sara recognises him as he leaves the elevator. Probably late thirties – older than his social media profile picture, she notes. Nice hair, longish, some grey. He smiles as he spots Sara. Nice smile, too.

"Sara! How nice to meet you at last. I've been looking forward to your visit."

Not as much as I have, Sara thinks to herself, offering her hand and blushing. "It's nice to meet you at last, Professor. I'm so excited to be here but absolutely terrified about Monday evening."

Bamrung touches her lightly on the arm and reassures her that all will be fine, that his colleagues were extremely interested to learn about what she has discovered and that he will ensure that everyone is on their best behaviour.

"Come, let's get out of here. Some of my PhD students are going to meet us in a little bar just around the corner. We often go there for beer after work. They also do good traditional snacks. You like Thai food, I hope?"

Sara confesses that she isn't very adventurous when it comes to food and hasn't in fact ever tried Thai food (embarrassing) – but that she wants to try as much as possible while she is in Bangkok (scary).

Sara and the Professor chat while crossing the quiet university precinct in front of the history department to the unassuming Phraya Lounge, she about her life in London, he about his life in Bangkok. She rapidly compiles a mental list of useful facts about him. He appears to be single, or at least unmarried, and lives in the west of Bangkok, on the other side of the river. He has no children. One brother who lives overseas. His parents both died in a road accident when he was an undergraduate student. He clearly has a good sense of humour, enjoys food and music, and rides a motor scooter to work.

Bamrung, without her realising, is also compiling a set of facts: Sara is also single, very attractive (awkward), probably twenty-two (damn it), an only child, clearly nervous (he can work on that). Very intelligent. Needs to see the world. What a place to start.

Bamrung introduces Sara to two of his PhD students, already sitting outside the Phraya Lounge on plastic chairs. "Guys, this is Sara, just arrived from London. She's here to present some of her work to us. I'm sure you're going to be fascinated."

One of the students, a Thai girl sucking on a bubble tea who looks far too young to be a PhD student, squeals with delight.

"Another girl! Yippee! I'm Linda, so happy to meet you!"

Sara shakes Linda's hand vigorously and laughs. The second student appears to be far more serious. Bearded, probably from India, Sara reckons. He stands to shake Sara's hand, bowing slightly. "Amar," he says, simply.

Sara settles between Linda and Amar and the Professor orders cold beer. Conversation flows easily. Amar speaks intensely and at some length about his PhD (a study of Siamese monastic farming records from the 16th and 17th centuries) before Linda interjects and talks with passion about modern Thai culture. Bamrung enjoys spending